## "I'm glad I'm incapable of loving that way."

Justin sounded angry. "Our mother died a few months after Kit's birth, and father blamed Kit. By the time I'd begun to reason for myself and realized that Kit could hardly be held responsible for our mother's death, Kit had turned in on himself." He shook his head sadly. "How do I recompense him for all that?"

"I don't know," Romney responded wearily. "But I do know that there is something you could do that would hurt him more than anything that has gone before between you."

"You're referring to yourself." Justins voice had grown silky and dangerous. "I think you're overestimating Kit's capacity to love. He's not like our father. It won't hurt him to lose you."

"No!" Now more than ever she had to ⬛⬛⬛⬛⬛⬛⬛⬛⬛⬛ truth.

**JAYNE BAULING** wrote for years before she found the confidence to let anyone see what she was doing. Now she writes full-time. But she still finds time to putter in her large untidy garden and breed sealpoint cats. Traveling, she says, is her obsession—so for her, real-life romance is often necessarily a long-distance affair.

## Books by Jayne Bauling

HARLEQUIN PRESENTS

These books may be available at your local bookseller.

Don't miss any of our special offers. Write to us at the following address for information on our newest releases.

Harlequin Reader Service
901 Fuhrmann Blvd., P.O. Box 1397, Buffalo, NY 14240
Canadian address: P.O. Box 2800, Postal Station A,
5170 Yonge St., Willowdale, Ont. M2N 6J3

# JAYNE BAULING

## thai triangle

*Harlequin Books*

TORONTO • NEW YORK • LONDON
AMSTERDAM • PARIS • SYDNEY • HAMBURG
STOCKHOLM • ATHENS • TOKYO • MILAN

Harlequin Presents first edition May 1986
ISBN 0-373-10879-6

Original hardcover edition published in 1985
by Mills & Boon Limited

# CHAPTER ONE

HE watched the young couple as they strolled towards him, welcoming the opportunity to observe them before they became aware of him. It might be spying of a sort—certainly Kit would think so and resent it—but he felt no compunction. Aware of being studied, the boy always launched himself into an act designed to deceive, to conceal, and especially to provoke, and it had been going on for too long. He needed to find out how much he was to blame for that self-destructive aimlessness, and how much was just Kit's volatile temperament, a combination of reckless hedonism and an appalling hypersensitivity which was cloaked with a perpetual performance of defiant indifference.

The beach was long and smooth, and they were taking their time, their pace unhurried, their few verbal exchanges obviously of a desultory nature. A lack of vitality was understandable in this heat. The Gulf of Siam had a glassy look, as broodingly still as if it were a painting in heavy oils, the distant small islands having the quality of an illusion, something not quite real, and the heat-hazed sky was sultry, heavily oppressive.

Not everyone was lethargic, though. The magnificently endowed Scandinavian woman who had smiled at him so beautifully when he had first stepped on to the beach sat up and donned her bikini top before striding down to the water's edge. He spared her glowing perfection another brief smile because any woman who could still look like that at her age, late thirties he guessed, merited only admiration.

Then his attention returned to the young couple, the only other people on the hotel's private beach apart from the Thai attendants who had tried to persuade him to go para-sailing just now. Most of the guests seemed to favour the swimming-pools scattered about the hotel grounds at this late afternoon hour.

Justin Faulkner went on watching his young brother and the even younger girl at his side. His brother . . . Who was the girl?

He had thought at first that Kit had acquired the companionship of a so-called Thai maiden, that fifty-percent accurate designation given by hotel staff members all over Thailand who never lost much time in notifying unaccompanied male travellers as to what was available for their pleasure.

She was as slightly built and graceful of movement as any Thai, and beneath a simple blouse she wore one of the long straight cotton skirts so many of the local girls still affected with that fine sense of what suited them best. Hers was fuchsia-pink with a broad band of golden embroidery, and beneath it her small feet were unshod. He wondered idly if she always moved so beautifully or if the narrowness of the skirt was forcing that daintily gliding walk. Her smoothly shining dark hair was also reminiscent of a Thai girl's straight and silken, the style very simple, shoulder-length with a deep fringe very slightly flicked, but now that the distance between them was lessened he could see that she had a European skin, creamy beneath the tan and with a faint hint of roses in her cheeks. It was a small exquisite face, delicate yet strong because the features were clearly defined, straight little nose and angular cheekbones.

He wondered where Kit had picked her up. Somewhere along the circuitous route he seemed to have taken from the Philippines to Thailand, a journey that had taken him a year—because she couldn't be the little art college dropout who had reportedly left England with him last year. He couldn't imagine any girl, however mercenary, enduring Kit's moods for such a length of time for the sake of his unlimited financial resources. For that matter, he couldn't imagine Kit not tiring of a girl after a couple of months. They were alike in that respect, one of the few things they had in common as brothers.

He stiffened. Kit had looked up and seen him, and Justin knew that the younger man's momentary immobility was a mirror image of his own frozen wariness. Time was suspended for those few seconds of caution and suspicion.

Dear God, he reflected with a sudden violent excess of exasperated feeling, how had they ever managed to come to this? His mouth curved grimly. At least the situation had never been exacerbated by a woman coming between them and was never likely to be. The difference in their ages was insurance against that ultimate, intolerable overloading.

Boy and girl were still standing there, a short distance away, their attitudes irresolute, but he didn't stir. They would come to him, eventually.

Kit's face, he noted, was empty of emotion and yet oddly vulnerable at the same time. Nothing had changed. He felt the old impatience wake in him, but it was arrested as he noticed the girl again, the graceful hand she lifted to touch Kit's bare arm, her lips moving as she spoke a few quiet words.

It was the merest touch and yet the tension went out of Kit quite visibly. Justin could see him fix the smile on his face as he flung back his golden head and strode forward.

He wanted to laugh. Incredibly, Kit had found himself someone to lean on. Even younger than Kit, the girl was palpably the stronger, supportive partner in the relationship, and he wondered cynically how long it would last. He would also be interested to know what had motivated her to assume such a rôle. Kit's affluence and a taste for a life of leisure and pleasure was the obvious answer, but she could be one of those women, the eternal martyrs, who attracted and were attracted to men like Kit, time after time without ever learning the lesson, men who required of them that they be mothers, not women.

She held his attention securely now, so that he barely noticed as Kit reached him. The lips gave clues, but they seemed contradictory. The mouth was delicately sculpted and yet wilful and ardent at the same time, tender and generous, passionate and compassionate, youthfully vulnerable and yet hinting at some inner strength and a long experience of self-control, as if something had set and hardened far too young ... But as he watched, Justin saw the lips tighten, with anger he thought, surprised, and then he saw the resentment sparkling in dark sherry-coloured eyes, resentment on Kit's behalf.

He turned to his brother, aware of an odd sense of disappointment. He had guessed it right. Kit has cast the girl in a maternal rôle and for reasons of her own, probably material, she had accepted it and had sublimated all other facets of her nature.

'Kit.' He could feel the tightness of his smile.

'Hullo, Justin!' Kit was employing that over-emphatic voice he had acquired before dropping out of RADA and his answering smile was brilliant and hard. 'Checking up on me?'

Justin looked at him. Kit had always been a pretty boy when he wasn't being petulant—He supposed that he should stop thinking of him as a boy. He was twenty-three, for God's sake, but he still seemed so young ... Less mature than this taut girl who was watching him so concernedly, and yet he knew she must still be in her teens, a virtual baby—and Kit's mother-substitute.

'You've had a year's grace,' he reminded him quietly.

'A year?' For a fleeting fragment of time, Kit looked haggard and Justin noted the girl's involuntary gesture—of denial or protest? Then his brother laughed. 'A year, a month, a week ... You've always thought in terms of time. I'm different.'

'And that makes you privileged?' He couldn't help the sarcasm and he noticed how the girl moved closer to Kit, a mother perceiving that her child is threatened.

'Go away, Justin!' Kit's voice was suddenly low and intense. 'I don't need—I don't want you here. I'm not going home, I'm staying right here!'

'If it was left to me, you could go to hell for all I care,' Justin retorted, already weary of the exchange. 'But our father was concerned.'

'How is the old bore?' Kit asked perfunctorily.

'As you say, old,' he said tersely.

'Well, go back and tell him I haven't taken to smoking opium or contracted—I'm sorry,' he broke off to add with what appeared to be genuine contrition as the girl touched his hand. 'Go back and tell him Romney keeps me on the straight and narrow.'

'Romney?' They couldn't guess how shaken he felt.

Kit smiled with some warmth and drew the girl into the circle of his arm. 'Romney, my brother Justin. Justin, let me introduce my good angel—among other things—Romney Channer.'

'I've heard a lot about you, Mr Faulkner,' she said with faint mockery, dark eyes flashing, but for some reason it seemed to distress Kit who grew tense again and, perceiving it, her expression became contrite.

'And I ... know a lot about you, Miss Channer,' he responded deliberately. 'I congratulate you on your staying power, and I wonder very much about the reason behind it.'

'Yes?' He could see that she grew wary, refraining from reacting before she understood him clearly.

'How do you know about her and what do you mean about ... staying power?' Kit demanded aggressively.

'A year, Kit?' he taunted. 'That's a long time for you. Romney Channer, a fellow student at that art college you thought you wanted to attend after RADA didn't live up to your expectations ... She left England with you a year ago.'

'How do you know all this?'

'Dad had you traced when you disappeared.'

'Typical,' Kit snapped. 'For God's sake, Justin, I'm twenty-three, not a child; can't I live my life as I please and in privacy?'

'If you persist in behaving like a child ...' He shrugged expressively.

Kit looked down into Romney's face. 'Are you beginning to see what I meant, my love?' he asked softly.

'I am, Kit. Oh, I am!'

She slipped her arm about his waist and looked at Justin with dislike, and suddenly he felt weary of the whole business. It was like confronting a pair of children who had united in opposition to the adult world to the point of refusing to hear reason, let alone consider it.

'Stop hating me, both of you,' he advised tiredly. 'I'm not here to make judgments or apply any pressure. I came solely because I still have some feeling for our father, although he'd hate to know that a major part of it is pity. He's old, he's tired and he has a lot to regret ... I told him I'd see you, observe you and let him know how you were, what you were doing. That's all.'

'So when do you leave to make your report?' Kit enquired with gentle malice.

Justin's answering smile was acid. 'Sorry to disappoint you both, but it's over eighteen months since I've had a break from work, so I've decided to take a few weeks off, and where better to spend them than here? I've always liked Pattaya ... I hope you won't let my presence inhibit you in any way.'

'We'll try not to,' the girl responded as if she had grave doubts about their success, and Kit grinned appreciatively.

Justin studied her with glacial speculation for a moment before glancing at his brother and making one last effort, as far as he was prepared to go at present: 'Come, you've claimed to be adult, Kit, and I'm sure Romney thinks of herself in the same way, so let's be . . . adult about this. What about a drink at the beach bar along there, and you can tell me about your travels in the last year? We weren't able to trace all your movements, you know.'

Kit shrugged rather sullenly. 'All right,' he said abruptly and, releasing the girl, turned and stalked in the direction of the bar, a slight slender figure in his brief white swimming shorts and a navy T-shirt.

Romney hesitated, then followed, her face composed beyond her years after a momentary betrayal of distress, and Justin remained where he was for a few seconds, watching the neatly economical gliding walk with a stirring in his loins that angered him. He had never before reacted thus to any of Kit's girlfriends and it was a complication he could well do without.

Seated at the bar, she ordered a Mai Tai, Thailand's most popular punch which included, among other things, rum and rice-whisky, but Kit opted for a soft drink.

'Be sure to include how Romney has reformed me in your report to the old man,' he taunted with a hard laugh and Justin saw the girl wince.

'I notice she doesn't practise what she preaches.'

A mischievous little smile played about her mouth, relaxing her and making her look very much younger. 'Kit doesn't need to drink, you see. He has me!'

'Both a stimulant and a tranquilliser.' Kit's sapphire glance softened as it came to rest on her face. 'Whereas poor Romney needs something extra to help her put up with me. I don't give you an easy time, do I, my darling?'

Her smile was melting. 'It was my own choice, Kit,' she said quietly.

Justin felt irritated. For a few moments, they were oblivious of him, speaking with their eyes in the way of very young lovers. He was mature enough not to resent having to revise his opinions and it was beginning to look as if some genuine and mutual affection at the least existed between the pair. They had after all been together, presumably lovers, for a year, and where Kit was concerned that was a phenomenal length of time. He ought to be relieved, it could be just what the boy needed, but irrationally he was angered, and this welling of annoyance was inspired by the girl. He felt an urge to challenge her, even hurt her, anything to provoke her out of her absorption in Kit. She was too wrapped up in him, hardly aware of anyone else, constantly alert on his behalf, distressed when he was distressed and ready to leap to his defence at any moment.

Impatiently, he suppressed the impulse to shock her into awareness of him. This was getting ridiculous. What was she? A girl in her teens who had probably initially been attracted to Kit by his unlimited supply of funds and the promise of a year's free holiday in the East, whatever she might have come to feel for him later . . .

'You dropped out of art college along with Kit, didn't you?' he probed when she looked at him.

'Yes.' She paused reflectively and shrugged. 'I don't suppose I'm any great loss to the art world. My ability didn't match my . . . the visions inside my head.'

'And yet you must have had some flair for them to accept you,' he persisted relentlessly and noted that Kit seemed more disturbed than she did by the point he was making. 'Has the ... sacrifice proved worthwhile?'

'There was no sacrifice involved,' she answered swiftly, eyes once more on Kit who was looking strained.

'How could there be? A dim and dusty old college versus the mystical, magical East?' It was Kit at his most theatrical but there was a harsh note somewhere there.

'You wanted that dusty college passionately at one stage,' Justin reminded him mercilessly. 'In the same way that you once wanted RADA and several other things I can think of.'

'I thought youth was supposed to be a time for experimenting,' Kit challenged sullenly.

'Youth, yes, of course, but isn't six years a little excessive?' Justin derided ruthlessly, and paused to allow the point to be taken before adding. 'Why the East anyway?'

But Kit had subsided in one of the sulky moods he remembered so well. He had never liked being taunted about his dilettantism, but Justin felt little compunction. It was time he grew up.

Romney gave him a reproachful look and answered his question: 'Why not the East, mystical and magical, as Kit has just said?'

'And squalid and sordid, but you don't see that side of it from luxury hotels,' he added cynically.

There was, he thought, watching her as she gave her attention to her drink, something quite incredibly erotic about the way she gently pursed her lips about the double straw and sipped the drink, eyes screened by dark lashes that cast faint shadows on her cheeks as she looked down at the purple orchids decorating her Mai Tai, absorbed fleetingly in an enjoyment that was quite simply and purely sensual. He felt something twist in his gut. The picture was almost innocent, even to his eyes, a girl enjoying a drink on a hot afternoon.

She looked up at him again, and he saw that her eyes were devoid of any awareness of his thoughts. It could be the self-absorption of youth, or the generation gap. He had seen children look at strange and unimportant adults in just such a way, incurious, almost indifferent, as if they weren't seeing anything that mattered or was real.

She spoke lightly, a child being polite to a grown-up, making an effort because Kit wasn't. He wasn't surprised. The bureau's investigations had shown Romney Channer to come from the sort of middle-class background where good manners and keeping up appearances were the cardinal virtues. And he supposed they were virtues. How many times had he heard her class described as the backbone of the nation, any nation? And so they were, particularly in times of trouble. They never broke down, they just went on enduring without ever betraying what it cost them. It was admirable, courageous—and frustrating, because you never knew what they were really feeling.

She said, 'Yes, well, it wasn't luxury hotels all the way, you know.'

'Tell me,' he invited.

'It would take a year!' Her smile was a courteous thing, warming only when she transferred it to the brooding Kit. 'Originally we were only going to go to the Philippines but when . . .' She stopped as Kit made some sudden involuntary movement. She gave him a reassuring look before resuming, but Justin could have sworn that a shadow crossed her face, some fugitive, barely noticed memory of pain, he thought, wondering a little. 'Well, Manila didn't offer quite what we'd been expecting, and we meant to go straight back to England. We had actually checked out and were on the way to the airport when Kit in his usual impulsive way said to hell with going home, why didn't we explore a bit of Asia for a while? We began with Pakistan. He said it was the logical place to start; I couldn't see it at the time but now I suppose that geographically it was logical, considering the route by which we've come. It was in Paki that he gave up drinking incidentally, after he had his bottle of Scotch confiscated. Hand it over or submit to arrest, they said . . .'

'So I handed it over,' Kit took up the story with a grin, his change of mood as swift as ever. 'I felt that if I was going to go to gaol it should be for something a little more exicting than the possession of liquor. Two dry months, and then when we moved on Romney got very bossy and said I'd proved I didn't need the stuff so why start again?'

As they talked, Justin studied both of them intently, noting the animation of their faces, the way their eyes became lit with enthusiasm at their shared memories. This way, he could almost like them both. They became people.

'Then India.' Romney paused dreamily, head on one side as if she sought for words good enough to describe something infinitely precious. 'We lived there for seven months and it wasn't long enough. We'd both seen the James Ivory film of *Heat And Dust*. We copied the girl in the modern section and lodged with local families in all the cities we went to . . . We also went to Nepal from there. Then we skipped a few countries where things aren't too healthy just now and came to Thailand. We meant only to stay a few weeks and move on, probably to Singapore, but I think I knew from the moment we stepped on to that Thai International plane and they pinned those orchids on me that Thailand would be something special.'

'For me it was those gorgeous air hostesses,' Kit agreed wickedly and she laughed.

'It's a purple country,' she supplied quaintly.

'Hasn't she got a darling way of putting things?' Kit demanded delightedly and Justin could see that real pride lay beneath his laughter. 'Purple passion! But you're right, my love, there's a lot of purple here . . . A royal colour, a royal country— and we've been treated like royalty ourselves.'

'And a country of orchids and butterflies,' she added.

'Especially the butterflies that come out at night,' Kit inserted irrepressibly. 'The Pattaya ones were busy when the U.S. navy called last week.'

'Your brother has a one-track mind,' Romney told Justin so indulgently that he was irritated again. Couldn't she be less of the doting mother?

'Yes, I'm surprised you didn't mislay him in a Bangkok massage parlour,' he commented sardonically.

'Oh, we didn't stay in Bangkok very long,' she replied, not reacting to his tone at all and he began to wonder if she was stupid.

'Romney wouldn't let me,' Kit teased with mock mournfulness.

'Liar!' she laughed at him and the added beauty it gave to her eyes was still there for Justin to see when she turned to him. 'On arrival in Bangkok,

Kit reverted to type and said it was time to become a member of the jet-set again, so we came down to Pattaya where we've been ever since, although we've been up to Bangkok for the odd day.'

Justin continued his inspection of them, endeavouring to sift through the evidence and draw some conclusions, but it was not an easy task. In so many ways his brother was still the Kit of old, petulantly prickly, selfish, provocative—warped with resentment. Yet there were certain major changes that he found hard to define. He looked at the girl assessingly. Had she wrought those changes, or was something else responsible? But what else could there be? Unless Kit had been dipping into the ancient religions of the East, but he didn't think it was that, because the old lack of tranquillity was still very much in evidence. Any serenity belonged to the girl.

He turned his head and found Kit watching him watching Romney.

Unexpectedly, Kit's smile was tentative, almost shy. 'We could ... I mean, perhaps a few weeks' break here is a good idea, Jus. You do look pretty tired.'

So did Kit, though. He had a frail, shattered look that angered Justin because looking at the girl's passionate mouth, he could guess what was responsible.

'Some of us actually work, Kit,' he said coldly.

'At being total bastards, Justin?' Kit had leapt to his feet, face flushed, and Justin saw that he was literally shaking with rage. 'You shouldn't need to push yourself, though. It has always come naturally to you, hasn't it? You're the true son of our father ... On second thoughts, find somewhere else for your well-deserved holiday, and I hope it's a hotter place than this!'

The few terms at RADA had taught him how to make a dramatic exit.

He was beyond the shade of the bar even before the girl was on her feet. Impulsively Justin clamped a hand to her wrist. Her skin felt as smooth and fine as a baby's.

'You're surely not masochistic enough to run after him when he's having a tantrum,' he grated. 'Or are you hell-bent on martyrdom?'

She gave him a startled look, then slowly resumed her seat, her eyes on her hand that was pinned to the counter because he still grasped her wrist. Almost, she seemed to have fallen into some sort of trance, he thought.

'He'll be all right ... Yes,' she whispered, as if reassuring herself.

Then she seemed to snap out of it, her mouth tightening to that too-old control as she twisted and turned her wrist within his encircling fingers. He felt the bittersweet needles of desire become active in him again and was disgusted with himself.

'That was cruel,' she said quietly as he released her hand and for a moment he wondered what she was talking about. 'He was trying to ... Kit was extending a ... Why did you reject him like that when he was making an effort to ... to bridge the ... the gulf?'

'Who are you trying to fool, me or yourself? And it's not a gulf, little girl, it's a great high wall that extends beyond anyone's power to vault, scale or dismantle, and it's built of the million and one wrongs my brother imagines have been done to him.'

'If they're imaginary then your wall is an illusion and you ought both to be able to step through it,' she retorted. 'Kit was trying to.'

'Yes? He allowed himself to sound sceptical, amused by her rose-coloured view of his young brother. 'Now why would he want to do that, I wonder?'

'Because . . .' She hesitated and it looked to him as if she were nervously considering the wisdom of answering him truthfully or otherwise. 'Because he was afraid that his earlier attitude might have made you decide to leave at once and . . . I think . . . he really would like you to stay for a while.'

'My God, love really is blind!' he laughed harshly. 'I'll be staying, you can depend on it, but believe me, Kit will be wishing me a million miles away for every minute of the time I'm here.'

'Yes, if you maintain this attitude, I suppose he will,' she conceded gravely. 'But you're the one who's blind, you know.'

She was looking at him and Justin gained the impression that she was seeing him for the first time, her mind finally removed from Kit for the moment. Her eyes wandered searchingly over his face without any self-consciousness. He found her inspection oddly impassive, as if she were unaware that he might be doing the same thing, assessing her, forming an opinion, and again he was reminded of a child looking at an adult, serious and considering.

'Do you love him?' he asked abruptly, but it was not what he had intended to say.

'Dearly,' she answered simply.

'Kit himself, not who he is or what he has?' He couldn't seem to resist probing.

'You're not only blind, you know,' she said calmly. 'You're also stupid.'

He found her lack of resentment disconcerting, and a rare cold fury was growing in him, directed at her, at himself and at Kit.

'Forgive me,' he drawled. 'You mean you're not benefitting materially from your association with my brother? I hadn't realised an art college drop-out with your modest background could manage to pay her share on a prolonged holiday of this type.'

'You know Kit is paying for both of us,' she said shamelessly, and there was a pause before she continued earnestly. 'But it's a fair exchange, you know. Kit is getting something out of it too, something he needs.'

'I can imagine,' he confirmed, sardonically meaningful, and saw that for the first time he had distressed her because the faint natural pink in her cheeks had spread and deepened to a dusky rose. She really was so very young, he realised, to have not yet learnt to be blasé about the relationship, but Kit was probably her first lover. Her embarrassment stirred him to uncharacteristic pity, incomprehensible because he had meant to hurt her and now out of mercy he turned the subject slightly: 'Does he love you?'

'Yes. In his way.'

She looked sad now and he knew she meant— insofar as Kit was capable of loving anyone other than Kit. All the same, he had to admit that it was something of a miracle, and not a small one, for Kit to have come to care for anyone at all, in any way whatsoever.

'You're probably right,' he conceded. 'If his description of you as his good angel plus certain other indications that have slipped out are anything to go by, then you certainly appear to have some influence over him. But you haven't been very ambitious in testing it, have you? The quit drinking rule is hardly original, and a favourite among your sex.'

'He doesn't smoke any more either,' she said and a gamine grin transfigured her face. 'Do I sound too terribly puritanical? Some of the so-called vices enhance the quality of living if they're not abused, but . . . Kit did . . . abuse drink . . . Only, there are other things that can be abused too. Influence is one. I would be abusing whatever influence I have over Kit if I persuaded him to take a course that wasn't ultimately to his benefit.'

'Ah, we come to the point, don't we?' he mocked. 'You're giving me a gentle warning not to ask you to persuade Kit to go home.'

'Yes.'

'Because to return would not be to Kit's benefit?'

'Yes.'

'Or because it wouldn't be to yours?' Justin couldn't resist taunting. 'Back in England, you might lose your hold on and over him. Your long holiday would be at an end and you'd have to find a job or go back to college.'

'They wouldn't accept me after the way I walked out,' she said flatly. She looked at him levelly. 'I usually say what I mean, you know. I said, to return would not be to Kit's benefit. I'm not involved in this.'

'How can you know it wouldn't be to his benefit?'

'What is there for him in England? A father and a brother who make demands he cannot fulfil.' It was no accusation, the way she spoke, merely a statement of fact with which she expected him to concur. 'Both of you have either blamed him or despised him all his life.'

'Is that what he told you?' Justin's lip curled.

'Yes, but it's what he refused to tell me that convinced me it was true.'

'My God!' He had been disgusted with himself for needling her, but now his disgust was turned against her. 'You just haven't got a clue, have you? You claim to love my brother and yet you fail to understand him. Haven't you learnt yet of his ability to distort—oh, so convincingly? He should never have quit RADA. He could make Dracula believable.'

'You're the one who fails to understand.' Beneath the surface sparkle, dark eyes were fathomless wells as a sigh fluttered through the passionate lips. 'How can two brothers be so far apart?'

'You can't be that naïve, Romney! Or can you?' he demanded. 'Obviously you have no brothers?'

'No, but I've a young sister for whom I'd die, and she'd do the same for me,' she stated with calm confidence and then fell silent.

Justin went on looking at her. It came as almost an affront to realise how little anger there was in her. It was incredible, appalling, that one so young could have lost the capacity for anger. With her safe, secure background, it was way out of the scheme of things unless she was some sort of changeling, because surely to God her experience of his shallow, selfish brother could not be responsible. Yet there was no doubting that lack of anger.

Instead there was sorrow. He could sense if flowing out of her and it was a conscious effort to combat it as he felt it streaming over him, but resist it he must, or it would engulf him.

She lifted the cerise stirring stick out of her drink and examined its three adorning orchids intently. Then she lifted her head and gave him a faint idle smile, as if there were no conflict, or rather, as if conflict were not worth the trauma of pursuing.

'Elsewhere, people sweat blood to rear orchids,' she mused slowly. 'They spend fortunes and develop ulcers. Here, they pierce them with a plastic spear and stick them in tourists' drinks. Poor, beautiful, exotic things.'

# CHAPTER TWO

ROMNEY put down her hairbrush and stared at her mirror image, reading her own thoughts from the reflected eyes.

He had been so cold. She had never met anyone so cold. She had shivered, literally, the first time she found those icy grey eyes resting on her—but she had been scorched later when his long hard fingers clamped about her wrist, and a knife had twisted in the pit of her stomach.

He had been so cold, and so tense. She didn't think he ever relaxed. Like Kit. Kit never really relaxed either, though he pretended a phenomenal laziness. The similarity between them had shocked her, but now she could smile, knowing how offended they would both be could they know that she found them so intrinsically alike.

She stood up to inspect her entire reflection and knew a quiet satisfaction because the short, slit sarong of palest lavender Thai silk, purchased and made up during one of their day trips to Bangkok, had a soft lustre that imparted a radiant glow to her skin, her eyes and her hair. She knew she was fortunate in being slender and dark because those attributes had given her a facile ability to adapt to the fashions of the Eastern countries they had travelled, but there were hours when she wondered if it hadn't all come too easily. In the same way, she had adjusted herself to become the person Kit required her to be, and sometimes she wondered if she had any real personality of her own.

It was easy enough to be Kit Faulkner's girlfriend, or to wear a sari, whether of white homespun or silver-shot puce, or a sedate Thai silk two-piece costume, but who was Romney Channer?

She didn't respond to the knock at the door, knowing that Kit would come in anyway. She had given him that right a long time ago.

She sank back on to the stool as he entered, smiling at his approaching reflection, her bright, beautiful boy.

His beautiful mouth was hard, compressed.

'What did you make of him?'

She said cautiously, because she was always careful of what she said to Kit: 'I began to understand much of what you have told me.'

He smiled lovingly then at her formal phrasing and placed his hands on her shoulders. 'He's utterly invincible, isn't he?'

He could not know of the pride that was blent with the resentment in his voice, she thought.

'No.' Even for Kit, she couldn't be other than honest. 'In his way, but it is a different way, he's as fragile as you, Kit.'

'Fragile!' he echoed scornfully, but his laughter was uneasy and his hands tightened on her shoulders.

'Has he always been so repressed?' she asked.

'Justin, repressed? Now I know all those Mai Tais have got to you, Romney, my love.' His laughter edged towards uncontrol. 'We're talking about Justin, my big brother who has done and acquired whatever he wanted, all his life. Nothing stops him, and certainly not any inhibitions, because he hasn't any.'

'That's not quite what I meant. It's just that

everything is so contained in him, he's self-contained. He doesn't reveal any emotion. He works at making us react, betray ourselves, but he never expresses his personal feelings as a counter.'

'That's because he hasn't any of those either,' Kit retorted with a short laugh.

Romney gave it up with an indulgent smile. Kit couldn't see, any more than Justin could, probably because neither of them wanted to. Each had grown too comfortable with his distorted perception of the other to want to expend energy and emotion on a possibly painful re-think.

Because she knew she was right. Justin Faulkner possessed emotions that were buried deep, deep inside him and to which he never gave expression, and it was that which made him dangerous. When feelings were confined like that, the pressure built and built, until they burst free of the self-imposed restriction in a terrifying, coruscant explosion that could only be destructive to himself and to anyone else who was around when it happened, as finally and inevitably it would.

In the mirror she saw the haunted insecure expression that moved over her face like the shadow of a racing cloud. She didn't know how she knew, or why she should have such a sure knowledge of someone she had only just met, although she had known him through Kit's resentful eyes for a year, but the conviction permeated even her bones. She had a feeling that was certainty, that she and Kit were going to be there when the detonation came, caught in the ensuing conflagration. Presumably Kit would be the catalyst, because the long hostility of the brothers was approaching flashpoint.

Kit saw or sensed her momentary insecurity and

caught the infection. Dropping to his knees beside the stool, he said in a tone that was only just the safe side of panic: 'Keep me safe, Romney.'

'Yes,' she said automatically, twisting round to draw him into her arms while she wondered—who would keep her safe?

'Don't let him get me,' he urged, shaking.

'No.'

Her hands smoothed the tense back muscles and she kissed the bright head that lay just above her breast and then rested her cheek briefly against it as his arms came round her waist convulsively.

Romney lifted her head again, but their reflected images were more than she could bare to see, accusing, reminding her poignantly of just how their relationship was weighted, so she looked down again, seeing the short golden hair, bright and clean, still slightly damp from the shower.

Kit was a golden boy. He had everything—and nothing. Although nowhere near as tall as his brother, and slenderly built, he was perfect, with his brilliant hair and sapphire eyes, that beautiful mouth and fine delicate features. Once she had thought him too pretty, in the days when his skin had an almost effeminate peach bloom, but that was gone now although his deep golden-brown tan concealed the truth, and there were tiny lines about the mouth and eyes, and smudgy shadows too.

It was difficult to remember the days when she had disliked him. He had been slightly older than most of them at the art college, yet still he had been the archetypal vision of gilded youth, spoilt and charming and, for Romney, too exotically flamboyant to interest her. He had done and said outrageous things and for some of the girls that had been part of his attraction, as had his background which had been common knowledge among them: the legendary wealth and ability of the father, finally overshadowed by the attributes of the older son whose flair and acumen had enabled them to expand until they were a major power in every facet of the business world and not just the airlines and hotel groups with which they had begun. Then there was Kit, the romantic rebel, the black sheep who had taken up several supposedly glamorous careers and put them down again soon after, like a child with too many toys.

The boys at college had always disliked him, even more so after they had been forced to abandon their initial malicious opinion by the evidence that Kit was definitely heterosexual. He stole their girlfriends, but only for a week or a month, which made it even worse, because there was never any real need involved on his side. The girls had been divided into three groups: those who had already suffered at his hands and learnt to hate him for the smarting pride or ruined lives which was all he left them with when he had finished wreaking havoc in their hearts; those who waited their turn to become his victims, undismayed even by the trauma undergone by one of their predecessors who had walked into class, her face contorted with anger and pain, and tried to physically attack Kit the morning after he broke up with her; and those who watched and learnt to despise their own sex almost as much as they did Kit.

Romney had been one of that last minority group, priding themselves on their intelligence, and she would have continued so but for her inability to walk past suffering. That still stood out as the turning point, the day she had found him seated alone in the college canteen, shoulders hunched, eyes bloodshot in a pale, drawn face. She had thought at first that he had a hangover, but then she had seen that his lips were quivering like those of a small boy who has lost his mother.

Now she was bound to him with the strong bonds of her own compassion, but she had learnt too to love him.

Kit stirred in her arms, drawing her back to the present.

'Justin came to see me a little while ago,' he murmured against her warm satiny skin.

'Oh. I thought you wouldn't be talking to each other after the way you parted this afternoon.'

'Oh Romney!' He laughed faintly. 'A minor altercation like that? You haven't seen anything yet. But we always speak to each other again.'

'Yes, I suppose it would be a very unsatisfactory sort of hatred if you had to be silent and never express it,' she teased, but the way he stiffened warned her that he was unamused, so she added, 'What did he say?'

'Well, first he mocked us for being so coy as to have separate suites, so I said even lots of married couples prefer to sleep apart and he said yes, marriage did that to people.' Kit seemed to think his brother had said something rather clever.

'He's very cynical, isn't he?'

'Yes.'

'Like you.'

'I'm not cynical about you, though, Romney.'
His voice was muffled. 'You're the one thing I
believe in. Justin doesn't believe in anything.'

'Poor Justin,' she commented lightly.

Kit jerked away from her as if stung and looked
up at her with bitterly blazing eyes. 'My God!' His
laughter was harsh. 'Perhaps my father would be a
little less conceited if he knew that both the sons
he has produced are so abnormal they can evoke
only pity in a woman like you.'

'You know that's not true, Kit. It's not all,'
Romney soothed. 'You know I love you.'

'Now, yes.' The beautiful mouth twisted. Then,
shamefaced, he dropped his eyes. 'I love you too,
Rom.'

'Yes.'

'And I need you.'

'I know.'

There was a short silence before Kit straightened, saying, 'He wants us to have dinner with
him.'

Romney felt a cold dismay creeping over her.
She wasn't ready to face Justin Faulkner again,
but she knew Kit needed her at his side to be able
to do so himself, and her duty was to Kit, a freely
chosen duty.

She stood up gracefully. 'I'm ready.'

Kit seemed as subdued as she felt while they
made their way to the central building which
housed the hotel's restaurants, a considerable walk
because the complex comprised a series of
buildings linked by passages, stairs and lifts, all set
in gardens rife with lush tropical flora. Every room
had a view over the Gulf of Siam and Romney had
never known anything so exotically luxurious in
her life. The hotel had its own private beach, and

every conceivable facility, and she still hadn't lost her awe although she had learnt to relax and enjoy all that was offered. Nevertheless, she still occasionally felt herself out of her element, an alien in a strange environment, because prior to the advent of Kit in her life she had only read about the sort of people who stayed here, the affluent from all nations, those who played all year round, following the sun, and those who worked and played and derived the greater pleasure from their leisure because of it. Now they seemed to accept her as one of them, simply because she was staying here with Kit.

Justin awaited them in the cocktail lounge of one of the restaurants and Romney made a fresh study of him as she and Kit walked towards him. He was tall and leanly built, but powerful. His clothes were elegant, the colours light to complement his own pale colouring. It was one of those strange contradictions that made nature so unpredictable, she reflected, that the weaker brother should have the richer colouring, although there were many similarities. Kit had once told her that Justin looked like their father, he like the mother whose death just a few months after his birth had occasioned so much conflict within the family in the long years following.

Justin's hair was ash fair and smooth, his eyebrows and lashes darker, and his eyes were an arctic grey, while his features were severely chiselled. He might have been carved of marble, so coolly devoid of emotion did he appear, and yet she could find in him too a stern male beauty, chill and utterly masculine.

So fair, so frightening ... Appalled, Romney realised she had been picturing him in his entirety, without the covering barrier of his clothes and with a sparking, stinging warmth welling in her loins-and gathering in heat. A hot, scarlet tide of shame spread through her and she felt sick, her legs barely capable of carrying her forward. She knew she could not look to Kit for any support or protection, because she was here to protect him. It was the way of things and she dreaded his reaction if he ever guessed how his brother affected her. With an inner effort she composed her face and was able to greet Justin with a slight, vague smile, but she wondered how long she could keep it up.

Some of the strain she had feared was, however, obviated by the fact that Justin had already made the acquaintance of Torben and Helle Elstrom, a wealthy Danish businessman and his wife, and invited them to join them for both drinks and dinner. The good-natured couple filled any gaps that might have occurred, since the big jovial Dane was in holiday mood and inclined to be ponderously skittish, while his remarkable wife flirted happily with Justin.

Leaning forward and kissing Romney's cheek, Kit murmured wickedly, 'If old lusty-and-busty can't mellow Jus then nothing can.'

For once, Romney was unamused by the title he always gave Helle. 'She must be a good half dozen years older than him,' she whispered coldly.

'But does she look it? I ask you?' He grinned. 'Do you think she has had anything lifted?'

'No, it's healthy living and good clean fun that does it,' Romney relented, giggling.

'I'm glad you said clean. Think about it, darling,' he murmured against her ear, his arm about her shoulders. 'Or do you want to be a raddled old bag by the time you're twenty?'

Romney drew away from him, her cheeks warm. She had thought his amorous moods a thing of the past; that they had progressed beyond that stage long ago; but she supposed his brother's presence was responsible, instilling in him a need to assert himself and prove himself as much a man as Justin.

Torben Elstrom wagged a playful finger at them and beamed indulgently. 'Young lovers! Romney fears you are embarrassing us, Kit.'

Romney stretched her lips into a smooth smile, aware of Justin's pale glance flickering over her. 'Yes, not in front of the grown-ups, please, Kit,' she adjured mischievously and they all laughed, but Justin's eyes were cold and she knew with a pang that she had also discomfitted Kit and, it appeared a moment later, set him up very neatly.

'Quite,' Justin agreed with something of a snap. 'I'm just surprised Romney had learnt it before you, Kit. Public displays of physical affection are so very, very young.'

'I'm surprised you can remember things like that, Justin,' Romney tried to make amends, her manner languidly impassive, and to an extent she succeeded because Kit grinned and relaxed.

'And so is that sort of challenge, darling,' Justin drawled coolly. 'My mistake. I had begun to think you were more mature than Kit.'

'One of many mistakes; or does this mean a whole new experience for you?' she enquired gently, hoping to disconcert him because he was far too suave and self-assured.

'It means, little girl, that I must learn to curb my optimism and not hope people are other than they appear to be.'

He didn't give her a chance to retaliate, turning at once to say something to Helle.

Thereafter, until they went in to dinner, he ignored her, but as they all hovered in the small commotion caused by Helle thinking she had mislaid her handbag and Torben's teasing, Romney found him beside her, and long fingers touched her inside arm lightly and coolly.

Startled, and shamed by the immediate weakness, so sweet and warm, that assailed the lower part of her body, she looked up at him.

'I'd like, some time, to show you just how much I remember, Romney,' he said softly, for her ears alone. 'I remember things you haven't yet learned, because I doubt if Kit has taught them to you.'

She drew her arm away and contemplated him silently for a few seconds, eyes growing velvety soft and said as her mind absorbed the body's instinctive knowledge of what might have been, but which it knew must never be.

'And I'd like it if you wouldn't,' she said quietly. 'Kit is your brother.'

'Do you think that would stop me?' The grey eyes glittered coldly.

'I would hope that it would, and not only for Kit's sake.'

She moved to where Kit waited for her, eyes suspicious as he watched her.

'What was that about?' he asked sharply as she reached him and the hand he laid on hers was cruel.

Her choice—her sacrifice—made, Romney could look at him with peaceful eyes in which he might read only her love for him, and a small sigh escaped him.

'Shouldn't you tell Justin, Kit?' she ventured calmly as they walked to the table.

'No!' The word was like the crack of a rifle and the tortured sapphire eyes were wild. 'No, Romney! I'll . . . I'll kill you if you ever give him a hint. It has to be my way, the way I want it to be. It has to be! Don't you understand?'

'It's all right.' She touched his shoulder and left her hand there until she felt the trembling tension leave him. 'Yes, love, I understand.'

She understood his need to meet his brother on as equal terms as he might, but it didn't stop her being desperately afraid. She felt cold with fear and pity. They were storing up so much pain, these two brothers, and it could become unbearable agony if she were weak.

And she couldn't, oh, she couldn't be strong for both men. She wasn't really a strong person at all. Only Kit's need had forced her to become strong, but it was an assumed strength, unnatural to her.

'Are you all right, Romney?'

She looked up and found Helle staring concernedly at her from across the table, the seemingly endless joking suspended immediately she saw a fellow-creature truly troubled. 'Fine, thank you.' Romney smiled placidly, hiding the desire to weep. 'Just . . . a moment's homesickness, I think.'

Helle was nearly twenty years older than her, old enough to be her mother, and she thought that had she been alone with her in this moment of weakness, she might have confided in her. A woman would understand; a man, never. If she had learnt any lesson today it was that men were stupid, helpless creatures made needlessly cruel by their terror of showing their feelings.

Quite suddenly, she wanted her own mother, very badly. And her father and her sister, and home. She had been so long away and now England and, more particularly, the old home of her Surrey childhood, seemed infinitely precious.

Romney was, after all, a very human girl. There had to be moments of self-pity and now she thought it all out in conscious words—I'm only nineteen and far away from home, and there's no one and nothing to guide me except instinct, because of my promise to Kit.

She had made that promise, and now she knew he meant to stay here in Thailand. As a country, it suited him, as exotic as he was. Thai, beautiful Thai, as they said . . .

After dinner there was desultory dancing on the small polished floor to the romantic sound of a superb band which played softly enough for those who wished to converse rather than dance to be comfortable. Romney danced with Torben, or rather, was steered about the floor by him, for he was a big bearlike man, and then with Kit, and both times she watched Justin dancing with Helle.

She knew it was wrong and could only make the ultimate destruction of them all an irrevocable shattering thing, but she wished and hoped, she prayed, that Justin would ask her to dance. Just once, so that she might know what it felt like to be in his arms, all she would ever know.

He did ask her, a little later, when Kit had saucily told Helle it was time she danced with a man of her own age—himself!

Initially, Justin made no reference to his earlier threat, yet Romney felt it immediately she stepped into his arms, whether it was deliberate on his part or not. Their bodies were barely touching, and yet she was more acutely aware of him than she had ever been of anyone in her life. Her skin burned as with a fever and she knew she was trembling, both inwardly and outwardly, and she wondered if he knew it too.

He said calmly, 'Tell me again, so that I can be absolutely clear in my mind about it, that you will not use your influence to persuade my brother to go home and perhaps find some career that he won't abandon after only a few months.'

'It would do him no good and it might even harm him.' She had spoken quietly to begin with, but suddenly the vital importance of what she said put passion in her voice and caused her eyes to glow. 'Oh, please believe me and leave him alone in that respect, Justin. Talk to him, rather, in general terms, find out how he feels about ... about things, and you'll see what I mean.'

'You don't mean talk to him, you mean listen to him. Listen to the hysteria and melodrama with which he invests every simplest issue.' His lip curled and he was silent for a few seconds. 'Have you heard of Peter Panism, Romney?'

'It's a fashionable phrase, but are we still talking about Kit? The analysts usually apply it to men older than you are ... men of Torben's age, about.'

'Kit is suffering from a form of it too. He won't grow up!'

'No, he won't.' For once she sounded bitter. 'Why can't you just accept that?'

'For myself I can accept it quite easily,' he

responded harshly. 'I don't give a damn what Kit makes of his life, but it's worrying our father.'

'Your father is old, Justin, he has had his life and made his mistakes.' She couldn't afford to pity an old man when her bright, beautiful boy commanded all her compassion.

'And you're saying let Kit now make his? Fair enough,' he said, surprising her. 'But he's twenty-three, Romney.'

'We're well aware of his age.' Again, she couldn't prevent the bitter inflection.

'And you can claim to love someone like that?' he taunted. 'Or perhaps you're that way yourself. Perhaps you don't want to grow up and take the sort of responsibility which will leave a gap at your going ... Do you want a life that's a perpetual round of leisure and pleasure? Of course, Kit can give it to you.'

'Because you and your father have never stopped his allowance. Is it guilt that makes you keep on supplying him with funds?' She meant to hurt him, having guessed that particular truth long ago, but beyond a cold glimmer of rage in the grey eyes, his face remained impassive, and she sighed. 'Sorry. I shouldn't have said that, but you're judging me wrongly, you know. This isn't the way of life I would choose for myself.'

'It's all for Kit's sake, of course?' he drawled sceptically.

'Yes.'

'Do you really love him?' It sounded as if he quite genuinely couldn't credit it.

'Yes.'

'I don't think I believe you.'

Romney made no protest. Like Kit, if he had

made up his mind about something, there could be no changing it.

Justin drew her closer and the response of her body to the heat and hardness of his was a shocking thing. She felt as if she became congested with desire; her blood turned to wild, sweet honey in her veins, its course slow and sluggish, and she knew that a flush lay over her body. She was no longer truly dancing but moving against him in an erotic rhythm she had not realised she knew. Her hips seemed to have a new mobility, almost rotatory, symbolic of submission, an invitation to possession, and as the honey-feeling heated and quickened, her breathing grew shallow and rapid and she sighed and could have moaned aloud at the intolerable burden that had come upon her. She felt strangely heavy, weighted with the slow pounding need that awoke in the secret centre of her femininity and with the sorrow that lay in her heart, because ultimately there must come a denial.

What Justin felt, she could not guess. His movements might have been in response to the music or to her. She didn't know. She only knew they inflamed her senses and when he danced her out on to a verandah, she could make no protest.

Two handsome young Thai waiters were exchanging confidences in a corner, but they were left behind as Justin steered her round another corner. A sultry purple sky arched over the Gulf of Siam and the air was still and hot.

'No,' Justin said. 'You don't love Kit.'

'I do, you know.'

'How can you, when you want me?'

She felt the heat that flooded her cheeks and even in the darkness she couldn't look at his face.

'How can you know that?'

'By this.'

His hands dropped to close round her hips and she gasped and shuddered as he drew her relentlessly up against him, and even then, humiliated as she was, she was unable to prevent the involuntary writhing of her hips in response to such intimate contact.

After a moment, Justin's hands moved round behind her, one to remain at the small of her back, exerting pressure so that she was brought even closer to him, the other sliding up to the fragile nape of her neck, long fingers spreading upward and twining in her straight silken hair.

Romney's face was turned up, her lips parted as she awaited the touch of his, and the helpless heaviness seemed to be growing in her, weighting her eyelids and closing them, and making her breasts ache as they thrust against the hard wall of his chest.

'Justin,' she murmured lethargically.

'Yes.' He was quiet, coldly controlled.

She felt the tip of his tongue slide experimentally along her lower lip and a high, shivering little cry escaped her. It was instant bewitchment and she came to vibrant, urgent life in that moment, racked by the pleasure and pain of desire. Her slim arms went up to cling, her fingers closing convulsively in his ashen hair. His arm moved about her waist, tightening, gathering her in to him as his mouth covered hers completely and his tongue slipped beyond her sensitised lips to the warm moist inner flesh and made it a paradise.

Romney shook, her thighs trembling against the suddenly straining hardness of his, and her mind seemed to become filled with a clear, brilliant light, enabling her to know all the answers. This, this torrid, pulsing excitement, was what she had been created for, Justin the man she had been born to await unawakened and now find. He brought her to wild, wondrous life, his kisses deepening, becoming searching, in quest of her very soul it seemed. She knew she had never truly been alive until now.

Justin was shaken by a taut spasm and Romney felt him swelling and swelling against her with a fierce mounting of her own passion. She moved frantically against him, wanting, needing to be closer because now she knew that her only task and joy in life was to accommodate that driving central force that made him a man.

She arched against him, her hips quivering jerkily, and a faint protesting groan came from Justin, but those other sounds were coming from herself, she discovered with a sense of shock, hearing the choked little moans of animal need and unable to stop them because they were dictated by that exquisite, hot melting sensation deep inside her that had its area of greatest intensity where she was a woman.

She felt as if she were being deprived of her life-force when the kisses stopped.

'Justin, please!' she whispered brokenly and then his name became a feverish murmur on her lips, spoken over and over again as pleasure was renewed and she learnt of greater, intolerable heights of desire.

His lips were hot, grazing her neck and throat as he bent her back over his arm and ran his free hand over her body, exploring the extent of her arousal, discovering the painful rigidity of her breasts, the pebble-hard peaks thrusting up against the silk of her sarong.

A long, softly sobbing whisper of total surrender sighed through her lips as his hand moved on, down to where her thighs formed a vee, and applied a gentle pressure that maddened her senses beyond endurance.

But then, in the next instant, Justin was flinging her away from him, so violently that she staggered, catching at the balcony rail to steady herself.

'Justin . . .' She extended an appealing hand, unable to believe that it was over, and the return to earth from her first glimpse of realms of rapture was something that hurt. She arched, unbearably.

'That's all, Romney,' he said in a cold, harsh voice that shocked her after the melting heat of their embrace a few seconds ago.

'But . . .'

'Now I know.' He laughed faintly. 'I wondered about you, what you were made out of, and now I have the answer. Nothing so very rare or special at all. You're just another little tart to whom a man is only a man, never mind his name and face. You claim to love my brother, and yet you can be aroused like that by me—and by anyone else too, I imagine.'

The accusation, after what they had just shared, was initially incredible, yet as she stood there trying to read his face in the glowing purple darkness, Romney began to understand what she had done. She had made . . . She had made everything that much more intolerable.

And she couldn't even defend herself.

She turned towards the stairs a little further along the balcony.

'Please tell Kit I've gone to my room,' she requested dully.

'Shall I tell him to hurry?' Justin taunted softly.

Romney walked away without answering. Later it would worry her intensely, but at that moment she didn't care what he might tell Kit.

All that mattered was that she find some solitude in which to recover from the agony of the irrevocable. She supposed it had been inevitable that she should be caught in the brothers' conflict. Now they formed a triangle, she and Justin and Kit, but otherwise nothing was changed, because so much existed that was unalterable.

Nothing was changed, but everything was worse.

# CHAPTER THREE

THE telephone beside her bed woke Romney and she sat up, reaching for the receiver with a thudding heart, the remnants of a strange disturbing dream still curling like frail dispersing vapour in the dark places of her mind.

She had been lying in Justin Faulkner's arms and then she had looked into his face and seen that he had become Kit.

'Yes?' She sounded husky, and she located the light switch, wondering what time it was.

'Romney?' Kit's voice was a thin thread of sound. 'I'm sorry to wake you ... My head! Oh, God, Romney ...'

'I'll be with you in a moment,' she said calmly, putting down her watch. It was two o'clock.

Reaching for the crimson silk robe Kit had bought her in the Philippines, Romney's foremost feeling was a sense of relief. Kit couldn't know—Justin hadn't told him what had occurred between them, thank God! The fear that he might have done so had tortured her cruelly a couple of hours ago when she had been trying to fall asleep. She hadn't seen Kit again after returning to her suite; he had not looked in to say good night and she had not sought him out either, knowing she was too cowardly to bear what she would see in his face if it did happen that Justin had told him.

The corridor was deserted, softly illuminated by the lights that burned at intervals along its length, and a brighter light showed at the approach arm where the night floor clerk was at his desk.

Kit's room was next to hers, so there wasn't far to go, and as usual he had left his door unlocked.

He lay in a tangle of sheets, and his eyes were hazy and unfocussing in his grey face, his hair wet with perspiration despite the air-conditioning.

Seeing him thus, her regret at the way she had earlier betrayed his faith was multiplied and she bent to him, her sherry-coloured eyes concerned because the headaches were becoming more frequent.

'Have you taken your tablets?' she asked, quietly.

'Yes, but ... Oh, God, Rom, they don't help any more.' He was querulous, as fretful as a child. 'I can't stand it, I just can't take it any longer.'

'It's all right, I'm here.'

Somehow, although she had never had any nursing training, she had always been able to soothe him when he had one of his headaches, and after a while she was able to persuade him to take a shower while she remade the bed.

'Stay with me, Romney, don't leave me,' he urged, clutching at her when he lay beneath the sheet again.

'Yes, of course.' She lay down beside him.

The wan ghost of his normal wicked smile flitted across his face. 'Why don't you get in properly?'

'Too hot,' she murmured lazily, and he laughed a little, quite affectionately, knowing it was an excuse.

She had rendered him many intimate services in the year they had been travelling together, but to lie in a bed with him, with nothing separating their bodies, was too personal, too much like a yielding up of the privacy and space that were hers alone, not to be shared with anyone save the one true lover. Mostly now he accepted it, occasionally he still protested.

Nevertheless, Romney put her arms around him and held him in the slack embrace of loving kindness, and he sighed and let his head droop into the warm, tender curve of her neck.

'I do love you,' he mumbled. 'Even when I'm foul to you, and I often am, aren't I? I don't know. Sometimes I can look at myself from a distance, you know, and then I think I must have been born evil or something. But most of the time I don't think ... I just know there's this ache inside my head and I'm frightened, and so I think—why should I be alone? And I make you suffer as well. Oh, God, Romney, it's so bad, and I'm all in the dark. I don't want to be alone, don't let me be alone!'

'You're not alone,' she promised gently, lifting a hand towards the switch of the reading light. 'Will you sleep, do you think? Can I put the light out?'

'Yes, if you want to,' he allowed, still in that weary, dreary mutter. 'It's not so dark when you're here. But I've still got my headache. Why? Why have those tablets stopped working?'

'You'll be better in the morning,' she assured him as the light went out, because there was no other answer.

'I'd better be.' He nestled closer to her. 'Justin and I have arranged a boat trip.'

'That's nice.'

Romney smiled tenderly in the darkness, knowing he was unaware of the pathetic note of eagerness that had displaced the dull fretfulness—a small boy looking forward to a promised treat, an outing with his hero, the older brother.

Oh, dear God, she prayed, overwhelmed by a surge of protective love for Kit, her arms tightening about him, let Justin soften towards him! Please!

'In fact, we've organised a whole day—simply messing about in boats,' Kit went on contentedly, but his voice was growing slurred now and he rambled on in the way he often did when the sudden sleepiness which usually followed his headaches came over him. 'That's what Kenneth Grahame called it. Did you ever read that book when you were a little girl, Rom ... about the Water Rat and Mole and the others?'

'Yes.' Her mother had read it to her, but Kit had not had a mother, and she doubted if Justin or their father would have read to him.

'And they saw Pan ... Do you remember that part?' He was half asleep already.

'Yes, I remember.' Her tone was low and indulgent.

'Romney ... What did you think of Justin, really?'

It was a conscious effort not to stiffen.

'Go to sleep, Kit,' she advised quietly.

'Yes. Don't go ...'

He slept then, but it was more than an hour before Romney did so. She held him, still, but for these few hours she was free of him, able to let her thoughts roam where they would, able to be weak for a while and yield to fantasies about Justin Faulkner who already obsessed her as much as he did Kit.

Only, there was no point in it all, because for tomorrow, and for all the days after which remained, weakness must be set aside because Kit would need her again, and she would become someone other than Romney Channer; her personal needs and desires must be put away and she must be the woman Kit needed her to be.

So, in the dark, she tried to teach herself acceptance. It was easy enough to accept what was, what had happened to her; the difficult part was accepting what must be—or rather, what must not be.

She could never betray Kit. There was no way out and even to seek for one would constitute betrayal.

In the morning, Kit remembered the unanswered question.

'You never told me what you thought of Justin?' he reminded her, returning to the bed with a couple of glasses and the bottled water with which the hotel supplied the mini-bars daily. 'Want some?'

'I should get back to my own room,' she said.

'Why? It's early yet.' He picked up his watch. A faint smile touched the corners of his beautiful mouth and Romney thought how strange it was that he should have mentioned Pan the night before because Kit reminded her of nothing so much as a satyr when he smiled like that, evilly beautiful and sadistically cruel. 'Stay and talk to me for a while. No-one understands me like you do, Romney.'

'All right,' she yielded easily, because it could do no harm and that was what she was here for anyway, to listen to him and pacify him.

'So?' he demanded, eyes bright as he watched her drain her glass, all shadow of pain gone from them. 'About Justin? What did you think?'

Romney concealed a sigh. 'I think that, as brothers, you're very alike, and yet very different too.'

'How diplomatic of you,' Kit taunted. 'But I meant personally, Romney. What did you think of him as a man?'

'Well ... he's a man,' she began cautiously, putting down her glass and shrugging uncertainly, but her eyes grew teasing as she looked at Kit, knowing he believed his brother to be a highly exceptional man. 'Just like any other.'

'Then why were you out on the balcony with him last night? What were you doing?'

The delicate pink tinting her cheeks deepened fractionally. 'He wanted me to confirm what I'd told him earlier, that I wouldn't try to persuade you to go home.'

She was bending the one truth, because they had still been dancing when Justin had asked her for that confirmation.

'I'm not stupid, Romney!' Kit's voice shook with temper. 'I saw how you danced with him ... And I know my brother. Yes, we are alike, you're right. He's just like me, or like I used to be, in the respect that he'll seduce any attractive girl just for the hell of it ... And so much the better if she happens to be my girlfriend, because such a victory would appeal to his competitive instincts. He's going to try to take you away from me, Romney, and you're going to let him.'

'No, Kit.' Pity mingled with her distress. 'No, love. How can he? I won't let him, I promise you.'

'Do you love me?' he demanded fiercely.

'Of course!' Romney's reply was fervent, and almost happy because it was a relief to be able to tell a simple truth.

'And you don't find Justin attractive?'

'Only ... from an aesthetic point of view,' she lied sadly, but to tell the truth would have constituted the greater sin.

'Then prove it to me!' Kit turned to her, his hands grasping her shoulders and pushing her back against the pillows. 'Let me make love to you, Romney. Now! This morning!'

'Ah, no, Kit.' She touched his face kindly. 'You know we agreed to leave sex out of it, and that's the way it has got to stay if you want me to go on being what I . . . have been to you.'

'But now, a year later, it wouldn't be what you said it would be. I wouldn't be reducing you to the level of an object like those other girls I've used . . . You know that, Rom. You know I love you. I said I wanted to make love to you, not have sex with you.'

'It's still sex, Kit, and it complicates things.'

His face grew sulky. 'Why are you sounding so kind and sad? Are you afraid I'll turn out to be impotent as well as everything else and you want to spare me the humiliation of failing? Believe me, I'm not that much diminished yet. I'm still quite . . . able, you know. I'll prove it to you. I want you right now.'

She didn't know what to say, what further protest to make without exacerbating the situation, and she lay inert as he began to kiss her. It even occurred to her that perhaps she owed him this as well as everything else, because he had so little, really, and she had so much.

But she couldn't make herself respond, her lips passive beneath his, and eventually she said regretfully, 'I can't.'

'No, because you want Justin,' he accused bitterly. 'But I won't let him have you. You're mine, Romney, you made me a promise . . . You must respond to me. I'll make you respond!'

His face was hectically flushed, his eyes glittering with rage, and his mouth was suddenly ugly as he kicked aside the sheet and flung himself over her. His lips were vicious, grinding against hers, tearing at them, and Romney wanted to weep for the ugliness and violence Justin Faulkner's advent had brought to the surface.

Kit wore only the cotton shorts in which he always slept, and now he dragged her already loosened robe apart and tore at the top of her white nightdress to expose one small but full breast, his hand closing greedily around it, fingers digging into the soft flesh, and the wry tragedy of it was that the pain he inflicted and her subsequent agitated fear could induce an ironic approximation of desire, the false first signal of arousal.

'I don't think you can love me, if you can handle me like this,' she whispered anguishedly.

A momentary flicker of shame in the sapphire eyes so close to hers was instantly suppressed.

'I'll be kind when you stop wanting my brother,' he advised jerkily.

Romney was wrung with pity, and sorrow seeped endlessly through her, a slow inexorable tide of sadness. This was what Justin had wrought with his presence less than twenty-four hours after his arrival. Kit's faith in her was shattered and he was lost and adrift again, as he had been when she had first known him.

But the assault was abruptly terminated when a loud knock sounded at the door. Kit leapt up immediately with a faint incomprehensible smile flickering about his mouth and strode to the door.

Romney lay back, covering her face with her hands for a moment, wondering what she could say to deter him when he had sent whoever it was away.

Then, to her horror, she realised he was opening the door wide and ushering Justin Faulkner in with an expansive smile.

'You agreed to eight o'clock,' Justin was saying tersely, but he stopped on seeing Romney, cold grey eyes flicking contemptuously over her dishevelment, his mouth twisting. Then, ignoring her, he turned back to Kit. 'I suppose it was too much to expect that you'd be punctual. I've told the man to hold the boat until nine-thirty, so you'd better move it if you still want to go. But perhaps a more seductive offer has arisen?'

'Oh, Lord, Justin, I'm sorry!' Kit was contrite. 'I honestly meant to be on time but ... Well, we didn't get to sleep until after two o'clock and then this morning ... I was delayed. You know how it is.'

Romney was sitting up now, having pulled her nightdress up into place as soon as she realised what was happening, but she knew those icy eyes had seen the evidence of Kit's assault, the faint finger marks beginning to show on her flesh, and that other shaming witness to what had been happening—but there was nothing she could do to conceal the fact that her mouth was bruised and her lip split by either Kit's teeth or her own. She kept her eyes lowered, unable to look at either man, her face, her whole body, suffused with humiliated colour.

'I know,' Justin confirmed sardonically. 'But you can't have seen the list of hotel rules in your dressing-table folder, Kit. Overnight guests, as they're euphemistically called, are required to have left by seven.'

'And not by way of the front foyer,' Kit laughed, then looked indignant. 'I think you might

be insulting Romney, Justin. She isn't one of the
butterflies who come out at night. She shares the
sunlight with me as well. She's coming out with us
today—aren't you, Rom?'

Romney couldn't answer. She stood beside the
bed now, tying the belt of her silk robe tightly
about her slender waist, her eyes on the floor.

'She's embarrassed, Kit,' Justin spoke silkily
into the silence. 'Or can it be that she's ashamed?
Of you? I know you've never welcomed advice
from me, but perhaps you'll listen to this, for
Romney's sake. Never, ever, mark your women,
boy. If they're not exclusively yours to begin with,
you won't succeed in making them so that way.'

'You bastard, Justin,' Kit said quietly and a
sidelong glance showed Romney that he had gone
pale.

'Yes, I know,' Justin agreed wryly and there was
another hiatus. 'Well, if you still want to do what
we planned last night, I'll see you—both—at the
front entrance.'

The door closed behind him, and neither
Romney nor Kit spoke for a while.

Romney walked to the dressing-table but she
couldn't face her shamed reflection so she moved
on, round the room-divider to the luxurious little
lounge, a vase of orchids on the coffee table, the
couch and chairs deep and comfortable. A french
window opened on to a bougainvillaea-draped
balcony and she opened the curtain and stood
looking bleakly out over the already hazy Gulf of
Siam.

'I'm sorry, Romney.' Kit's voice broke.

'You did it deliberately, didn't you?' she
challenged huskily. 'You looked at your watch and
you smiled. You knew he'd come looking for you.'

'Yes.'

'Why?' she asked shakily.

'Because I'm just as much a bastard as he is.' Kit spoke from close behind her.

'Oh, Kit.' Romney's voice cracked and her eyes blurred.

'Are you crying?' He sounded startled.

'No, of course not,' she choked vehemently. She wasn't supposed to cry. She was the strong one. 'But why, Kit?'

'I wanted to show him . . . that you belonged to me. And sex is the only language Justin understands, as it was the only one I understood until I knew you.' Kit paused. 'He means to take you away from me, Romney.'

'I told you—he couldn't,' she reminded him quietly.

'Yes, I think you really believe that, my dearest, most loyal Romney,' he said sadly. 'But—Oh, you've been an angel to me, but you're only really a human girl, aren't you? And Justin—is Justin.'

For Kit, it was an oddly mature view, but she only said, 'And so, to show him, to stake your claim, you set all this up? But what about me, Kit? Did you stop to think how embarrassed I'd be?'

It seemed no-one thought of her, because she wasn't really important. She wasn't a protagonist in the drama being played out by the two brothers; she was merely the bone of contention, hardly a romantic rôle.

'I really did have a headache last night, you know,' Kit offered in his own defence, returning to something like the Kit she knew.

'I know.' She turned and gave him a small smile.

'Are you very cross, Rom?' he asked humbly and she thought—he's only a baby!

'No.' She touched his shoulder, a little gesture of forgiveness. 'Just embarrassed. I think I'll go to my room now. I'll see you later, if you're sure you want me along. You know, it might be better if you and Justin went alone. You might reach some sort of ... of understanding, that way, if you could only talk to each other.'

'No!' he protested sharply. 'I'd say things ... We'd quarrel. I need you there, Romney, to keep me calm. I get upset when he ... Please!'

'All right.' She walked past him. 'I'll come.'

Already, she was becoming once more the girl he wanted her to be. She had trained herself long ago in obedience to his requirements, all personal inclinations subjugated to his needs.

'Why live like this if you're ashamed of it?' Justin asked coolly. 'Why let my brother turn you into a whore?'

The wind tugged at Romney's straight dark hair as she stood at the rail of the big launch, whipping her fringe back from her brow so that the once more serene purity of her face was revealed in its entirety. Her skin glowed, a creamy golden-brown, with little hidden away because she had abandoned the costumes of the East and was dressed with modern appropriateness for a day on the sea, having discarded her soft cotton shorts and top at the earliest opportunity in favour of a brief, simple hyacinth-blue and pink smallchecked bikini.

She said, 'I'm not ashamed of the way I'm living and, you know, Kit hasn't turned me into anything. I made a choice, a free choice, uncoerced.'

Justin stood beside her in charcoal-coloured cotton swimming-trunks. She had not intended spending even a minute alone with him, and initially she had been relieved to discover that the Elstroms and Otto Adelbert, the Swiss manager of their hotel, were to accompany them, although she had sensed Kit's disappointment. But somehow it had fallen out this way. Kit was now asleep in a canvas chair on the deck, face turned up to the sun, relaxed and vulnerable in repose, and their Thai captain had surrendered the piloting of the vessel to the adventurous Helle, watched by the other two men.

'I'm sorry you were embarrassed this morning,' Justin said abruptly, surprising her. 'My brother is not always exactly subtle.'

'You don't need to apologise to me for Kit,' Romney responded indifferently. 'You may have known him longer than I have, but I do understand him.'

'And I don't?' he challenged frostily. 'No, Romney, it's you who doesn't understand. If you did, you wouldn't be squandering yourself on him, because you wouldn't love him.'

'Is he so unlovable?' She had to remind herself that she herself had once despised Kit, and that most of the time he still wore the face and manner of the old, corrupt, destructive Kit. But Justin had helped to shape that selfish side . . .

'Of course, though, it's not really love that you feel, is it?' Justin was continuing musingly. 'I look at you . . . You have the face of a sweet submissive Madonna, or a dark angel . . . Kit called you his angle, his good angel, didn't he? And it's difficult to credit that all that motivates you is the venality of concupiscence. Do you know what I'm going to do, Romney?'

'Justin?' She looked up into the austerely

carved face and found the cool eyes remote but inexorable. His opinion of her was just one more thing to the multiple scourge, and there was so little defence she could make. Even to reiterate that she loved Kit would be pointless because, like Kit, once Justin had made up his mind, it took something cataclysmic to change it. The Faulkner men were not easily swayed.

'I'm going to take you away from my brother,' he informed her, his voice hardening. 'I don't much like you, in fact I despise you, but even you deserve something better than that selfish, malicious egotist can offer you.'

She closed her eyes briefly but could not shut out a vision of disaster to come.

'You couldn't,' she breathed, appalled. 'I wouldn't let you.'

'Couldn't I?' His smile was glacial, tormenting her. 'I think I could, Romney, and quiet easily too. I was halfway there already last night. Your appetites are almost entirely sexual, with perhaps a taste for leisurely, luxurious living as an accompaniment, so I shouldn't have much difficulty, as I can give you more than Kit can—more pleasure, I mean, I don't believe he knows how to pleasure a woman, only how to take pleasure, judging by the marks on you this morning and that broken lip . . . That's not my way.'

'Yes, well, every man likes to think that he merits the title of World's Greatest Lover, doesn't he?' she taunted with delicate mockery, smiling faintly. 'And he's usually aided and abetted in his conceit by his women, because my sex made a long study of the art of pleasing men before we woke up and demanded that men please us, and rule number one was—pander to his ego. Anyway, with the sex therapists producing so much literature, every man stands a chance of being as good as the next. You suggested it last night, remember? A man is only a man, you said.'

Justin was looking amused. 'Well, if that's true for you, I should have no difficulty whatsoever in depriving Kit of you.'

'And that's what it's all about, isn't it?' Romney's mouth had tightened. 'Taking me away from Kit. If I wasn't his ... girlfriend, you wouldn't give me a second thought.'

'Oh, I want you, Romney,' he assured her lightly.

'Well, you can't have me,' she responded steadily, ignoring the multiple pulses fluttering in different rhythms all about her body.

'I think I can. I could have had you last night, couldn't I?' He awaited her answer but when none was forthcoming he smiled cruelly. 'Because, in spite of all your theories about the equality of all men, I think you'd prefer my way to Kit's, else you wouldn't have been so embarrassed this morning. Let me show you.'

'No!' Her guilty, frightened eyes swung in Kit's direction as Justin picked up her hand, and he laughed shortly.

'It's all right, he's still fast asleep. The only way he could ever take being on the sea, however calm, without being violently sick was to sleep through it. He thinks no-one knows.'

Romney's heart contracted with sympathy for Kit, prepared to endure sea-sickness after his headache of the night before in order to show himself equal to his brother—in order to be with his brother, and Justin had spoilt his pleasure by inviting those others and was now openly declaring his intention to commit the ultimate in fraternal betrayal.

She asked impulsively, a little breathless because he still held her hand, 'Why did you invite the others, Otto and the Elstroms?'

'To distract Kit while I'm seducing you, should he wake up,' Justin laughed.

'Kit was right, you are a bastard.'

'Oh yes, we both are, in our different ways, but I think you'll prefer my way, Romney.'

His voice had sunk and softened, and she heard it as if experiencing a caress. He raised her hand to his mouth and his warm lips parted slowly over the smooth mound of flesh at the base of her thumb. As he sucked gently at her skin, Romney's fingers curled. Sensation was exploding in her like the irresistible uprush of sparkling bubbles when a champagne bottle is opened, effervescent and tingling, and her mind went blank, leaving her incapable of resisting. She felt Justin's mouth slide to a fluttering pulse and over the blue-veined fragility of her narrow wrist before his tongue probed the hollow of her palm, and sensation gave way to active desire, myriad fiery arrows sparking through her body, piercing her with the strange sweet pain of passion.

Somehow her free hand lay on his bare shoulder, trembling fingers curving into his flesh, and she looked at him and knew herself sinking deeper and deeper into the sensual spell as he nibbled gently at her fingertips.

'Ah no, Justin, don't! Please don't,' she gasped, drawing sharp shallow little breaths, half-crazed by his exquisite control.

'Why not? You like it and I like it.' His voice had roughened.

Too much, too much, she thought wildly, unable to tear her hand away or withdraw her eyes from his male beauty, the broad muscular shoulders, the hard chest with its covering of fine fair hair. His skin was tanned, although not as darkly as hers and Kit's, but he was still utterly, aggressively male, the most compellingly masculine man she had ever seen.

Justin held both her hands now, drawing them to his bare chest, and Romney spread her fingers wide, obeying an instinctive urge to touch and feel, to caress the hard flesh and stroke the fine covering of body hair. Justin stirred slightly as her small hands swept a slow circular pattern over his chest, but his face was tense, waiting.

Romney drew a shuddering breath. She was dissolving. Outwardly she was rigid, her stiff nipples straining against the fine material of her bikini, any movement she made uneven, jerky with the dissatisfaction engendered by the space still between them, but inwardly she was a churning, molten mass of wanting.

'When, Romney?' Justin asked tautly and waited for her answer.

Romney lifted one hand and laid her palm against his hard cheek as she looked into the cool unemotional grey eyes. Her own eyes were slumbrous and strangely serene as she finally faced temptation squarely. She stood poised on the very verge of surrender, almost tranquil because her yielding would ultimately bring peace and an end to all the uncertainty that troubled her mind and heart, and fretted her soul.

It was as if time were suspended and the world stopped turning. In those moments, between denial and acceptance, they scarcely breathed.

Then, somehow, Romney's gaze slid away from the expectant chiselled face and fell on the younger man who still slept, in sprawling golden beauty, in his deck-chair, and the choice was made. Not even to attain the paradise Justin had shown her could she commit the ultimate betrayal and take from Kit the improverished imitation of happiness he got from her. For her to gain rapture and peace, meant Kit losing—everything.

She took her hand away from Justin's face and turned from him, gripping the railing with both hands, staring unseeingly at the distant coastline.

'I can't,' she said tensely.

'Yes, you can.'

She could feel the heat of his body at her back and then his hands were at her waist, drawing her back against the hard length of him, and Romney sighed in helpless abandon. One strong hand spread over her ribcage beneath which her heart was pounding anxiously, the other trailed over her fluttering stomach and down, until he was touching her so intimately that she quivered and felt heat spreading all over her body.

She gasped and swallowed convulsively, striving desperately to retain mental control. Already she knew she had made an intolerable choice. A deep inner throbbing had started in response to the hand that held her so gently and so erotically, and she felt as if she were shattering into a million pieces under the strain of resisting the clamant urge to turn and submit to his silent, sensual demand.

'If you can't be merciful to me and Kit, then at least have mercy on yourself, Justin,' she beseeched raggedly. 'You'll destroy us all.'

'Dear God, Romney, if living with Kit has

warped your reason to that extent, then I am being merciful to you!' Justin exclaimed disgustedly.

'Justin! I can't be strong enough for—' Romney's frail control had finally snapped and she was incoherent. 'For pity's sake, let me go, leave me alone. I'm too weak to—'

'Yes, you are weak, aren't you?' Finally he released her and she heard the icy whisper of arctic snows in his voice, and it seemed to her as if he were speaking of her death and the hell that would follow. 'You make it almost too easy, but then I suppose that's what tarts are all about and how they get their reputation—through being easy.'

She felt too wrung out to respond, to defend herself, and anyway, Helle and the other men were coming round to join them, so she turned and drifted silently away on bare feet, going to where Kit still slept.

Her face softened, relaxing as she looked down at him and knew she had made the right choice, the only choice. He was beautiful and innocent in sleep, with no trace of the Kit who had explored the sordid depths and tasted the bitter dregs of human degradation at an appallingly early age, the Kit who destroyed people and put himself beyond forgiveness . . . This was simply her golden boy.

Something made her look towards Justin again and she found him watching her, his mouth curved in bitterly derisive mockery. Then he turned to smile at something Helle was saying and with a sense of shocked loss, Romney saw that his mouth could be as beautiful as Kit's when he relaxed.

But it would never be that way for her.

# CHAPTER FOUR

'DON'T say anything to Justin about the Philippines, Romney,' Kit warned from opposite her. 'He might start making connections.'

They had left their launch for a glass-bottomed boat close to one of the many beautiful little islands in this part of the Gulf. Kit had only woken up as they made the change, and he had hustled Romney towards one end of the long low craft, away from the others.

'Did he say anything to you while I was asleep?' he asked suspiciously.

'He . . . said he was sorry I was embarrassed this morning,' she admitted because he knew his brother well enough to be sure that Justin would not have ignored her completely.

'So am I,' Kit said quickly. 'Did he . . . did he try to turn you against me?'

'No.' She stared down at the fantastic coral formations and the colourful marine life darting about below the transparent bottom of the craft.

'Don't lie to me, Romney,' Kit advised sharply.

'Dear God, Kit, why are you worried if he did or he didn't?' she asked urgently, leaning forward and touching his knee. 'You must know that he couldn't succeed. You're hurting yourself, and me, and giving yourself needless anxiety if you can't trust me. I know you, remember, I love you, I understand you.'

'You pity me,' he added mockingly in the same tone.

Romney looked down again, her throat constricted. She knew that he loved her in his way, and that while her love and loyalty mattered to him and the loss of them would devastate him, the central issue was what Justin had said about him. She could have wept for them. In twenty-three years he had failed to win acceptance from his secretly beloved brother, and now it was nearly too late. Of course, in the crucial years when he might have succeeded, he had stopped trying, rejection leading to rebellion, a text-book case.

She glanced at Justin, down at the other end of the boat. Could he know what he had done? Certainly he couldn't guess how his unexpected presence was threatening the trust and tranquillity she had worked so diligently to build up in the last year.

'Stop looking at him,' Kit demanded jealously.

'Aren't we about due for another visit to Bangkok?' she ventured peaceably. If only she could get him away from Justin for even a day, she might be able to mend some of the damage.

'I suppose so.' Kit's eyes brightened. 'Perhaps Justin could come with us and we could stay there a night or two. There are things on offer in Bangkok that I'd like to experience, but only if I can share them with someone, and they're hardly suitable for girls like you, Rom. Did you know that eighty percent of all tourists to Thailand are male?'

Romney made a sound somewhere between a sigh and a laugh. She couldn't win!

You and me both, Kit, she thought drily. We're both obsessed with Justin.

It was Kit's turn to look at Justin. 'Look at him, simply getting browner and browner!' he exclaimed with rueful envy. 'I was hoping he'd suffer agonising sunburn and end the day looking like a fried farang.'

Romney giggled. Farang was the word Thais applied to Westerners, meaning guava, because that was what they thought they looked like.

She inspected Kit. His own tan was a deep golden-brown, emphasising the brilliance of his hair and eyes, but she thought she detected a greenish-grey hue tinging his face—sea-sickness, but she knew better than to refer to it.

Instead, she ventured: 'Kit, don't you think your ... headaches might be less debilitating in the more temperate climate at home? The humidity here in summer——'

'You traitor!' Kit's hand shot out to grasp her wrist, twisting it so viciously that she cried out. 'Oh, no, you weren't going to try to persuade me to go home. You told Justin that, you told me, and now here you are——'

'Kit!' Romney interrupted desperately because his voice was rising and Justin and the others were looking their way. 'What has he done to you, that you suddenly won't even permit me to feel concern for you?'

'Is that all it was?' he questioned sceptically.

'Yes!' Her voice was low and intense.

'I'm sorry, Rom.'

'I won't mention it again,' she assured him wearily, relaxing. 'But—at least take it easy today, love. It's less than twenty-four hours since you had that headache.'

'I can't!' He grimaced wryly. 'Justin is talking about snorkelling, and para-sailing, windsurfing, the lot!'

'You know you hate snorkelling as much as I do.'

They had tried it soon after coming to Pattaya and Romney had been frightened underwater, especially after acquiring several little black spines in her feet and calves from some little sea-creature. The Thais had rubbed the affected areas with lemon halves and told her it wasn't serious, but she had endured days of discomfort before they were all expelled. On the para-sailing issue, she and Kit were divided: she enjoyed it, but he, disliking most sports, loathed it as much as he did windsurfing.

'If Justin is going to do it, then so am I,' Kit vowed with the obstinate look she knew so well, and she subsided.

They were to lunch on another island and first they returned to their launch for a brief trip before being taken ashore by yet another craft with an outboard engine.

Walking up on to the beach, Romney turned to Kit who had been looking progressively unwell. 'At least have your aqua-scooter ride while you're still reasonably fit to enjoy it,' she suggested quietly.

On an aqua-scooter, his face took on the same wild, intensely absorbed look it had worn when he drove the sinister cream sportscar he owned in England.

'Yes, I might even do that now, before lunch,' he agreed. 'I'm not feeling much like eating, anyway.'

He and Torben Elstrom departed with a couple of young Thais a few minutes later.

Romney moved closer to Justin who was standing watching the various watersports going on off the beach. He had donned a pair of glasses with tinted blue-grey lenses and somehow they

made him seem even more remote and un-
approachable.

'Justin, may I ask you something?' she requested,
more nervous than he would ever know.

'What is it?' he enquired curtly, barely sparing
her a glance.

'Could you . . . if you would . . . opt for an
afternoon in the shade? Because if you go para-
sailing and snorkelling and all, Kit is going to feel
obliged to join you, and . . . Well, you know
yourself, the sea makes him queasy and . . . and he
doesn't really enjoy that sort of activity.'

She felt like a traitor.

'Then why can't he be honest and say so?' Justin
countered icily. 'Why must I give up what I enjoy
for his sake?'

'He feels . . . he has to do what you do, to win
respect in your eyes. It's a . . . hero-worship thing.'

Oh, Kit, forgive me, she thought.

Justin's laughter was harsh and disbelieving.
'Romney, don't try to persuade me to believe he
still feels some sort of little-boy compulsion to do
as I do, to emulate me. I destroyed that urge in
him years ago.'

'No,' she contradicted gravely. 'You destroyed
him, but you didn't destroy that urge.'

Justin regarded her contemptuously. 'I was
wrong, I think. You really are quite besotted.
Does he know what you're asking for his sake?'

'No!' Romney drew a quick breath as she realised
the risk she was taking. 'You won't . . . Please don't
tell him I asked, Justin. He'll be . . . upset.'

'And have another go at trying to break your
wrist?' Justin's mouth hardened. 'How can you do
it, Romney? How can you be so loyal to that
vicious, selfish boy?'

'You talked about destruction just now, Justin, but you didn't destroy anything—you created something.' Romney's throat was dry. She felt as if she were facing the devil and daring to insult him, but it had to be said, in fairness to Kit. 'Don't you think Kit was formed by you—and your father, years and years ago? You helped make him the way he is.'

'Oh God, yes!' Oddly, Justin seemed to relax, and yet he spoke with deeper emphasis of feeling than she had heard from him before. 'Do you think I don't wonder, every day of my life, just how far my responsibility extends? Just how much am I to blame, Romney?'

Startled, she looked up at him, but from behind the tinted lenses, his eyes were looking towards the misty, heatshrouded horizon, although she suspected that he was actually examining the past.

'Are you asking me to judge? Because I can't,' she said carefully, warmth stirring in her in response to the very human uncertainty that had been hidden behind the icy, self-contained demeanour. 'I only know Kit's side of the story and, blind as you may think me where he is concerned, I am well aware of his tendency to both exaggerate and distort.'

'No! No, I don't think I'm asking you to judge,' he sighed. 'We should all be our own judges.'

'I think that's a mistake,' she ventured. 'Because if we're honest, then we judge ourselves more harshly than we would others.'

'And if we're dishonest, we won't accept the full measure of blame that we merit,' he retorted with a faint crooked smile. 'And I have been both, torn first one way and then the other. But no, I'm not asking you to judge, Romney, just to tell me.'

'How can I? When I don't know. I don't think even you or Kit can truly know.'

'There are some things that are beyond doubt, though,' he went on, and she wondered why he was suddenly talking to her like this. 'Our mother died a few months after Kit's birth, as a direct result of that birth. Nobody told me that—I was nine years old—but I sensed from our father's rejection of Kit that he blamed him, and so I learnt to do the same.'

'You were only a little boy,' she inserted sympathetically.

'Our father wasn't, though.' Justin sounded harsh, but as he continued, his voice softened once more, taking on a note of tolerance. 'But he had loved our mother, completely and absorbedly, and he knew he was incapable of loving that way again. Poor bastard. I don't think he was ever properly alive again after she died ... Thank God I'm incapable of loving that way, or any way.'

'Then your father has made you, as well as Kit, an emotional cripple,' Romney commented and couldn't disguise her bitter regret for the tragedy that was so manifold, the tragedy of the father and the sons.

'It's not crippled to have a well-developed sense of self-preservation,' Justin retorted contemptuously. 'But we were talking about Kit, not me ... After a few years, I began to reason for myself and realised that he could hardly be held morally accountable for our mother's death. I was late in seeing it. Not as late as my father, but still criminally late because by that time Kit had turned in on himself. It was his turn to offer rejection. He was a farouche, ungovernable child, given to wild tantrums and sullen silences ... I tried, God knows, I tried, and so did our father to an extent, but more from a belated sense of duty than from guilt or anything else, I think. We met with no response; he was absolutely intransigent, and as he grew older and more unstable, he alienated us completely and we stopped trying . . . Occasionally, just occasionally, I could reach him, but now, I think, it's too late. He seems to have gone beyond my reach forever, but he has you now, and you've made him a little nicer, a little calmer . . . But that's what I need to know, Romney. What my brother has done, and been, and become . . . How far am I responsible?'

'And you can't ask him that, can you?' she probed gently.

'No.'

'Oh, Justin, don't blame yourself,' she urged impetuously, moved by the brooding way he spoke. 'You were only a little boy, influenced by your father . . . So much that makes or mars our lives is created in childhood when we're too young to know if we're working for good or ill, and how can we sort it all out years later? I don't think even the professional analysts ever discover every minutest influence. Even if you and Kit could sit down and dissect the whole past, you still wouldn't really know, because you have to take personality and temperament into account, and someone's mood on a given day, and then get back to what caused that mood. You can't do anything with the past, you can't rake it over or discard it or change it. You can only look to the present and start again.'

'How?'

She gave a rueful laugh. 'Are you asking me? How could I ever advise you?'

'Oh, I thought you knew all the answers,' he teased, not unkindly. 'You rationalise so very well.'

'Don't be silly, I know you can't really rationalise at all where emotion is involved.'

'But what would you do?' He really seemed to want to know, she reflected with some surprise, but she knew she couldn't presume to bear the responsibility of advising him when there were still so many areas of darkness.

'The only advice worth having is that which stems from experience and I've never in my life had to deal with anything of these dimensions,' she said quietly.

'You mentioned your sister yesterday. Do you and she never quarrel?' Justin smiled at her and Romney felt warmed by it—and weakened.

She laughed softly. 'All the time, but they're the sort of quarrels that can be mended with the offer of a loan of our best scent or favourite pair of boots. If they're more serious ... But I can't see you or Kit doing what Taormina and I do, I'm afraid. One of us will walk up to the other and put our arms round her and then it's all over. We don't talk about it.'

'Yes, you're right, it wouldn't work for Kit and me. We'll just have to work it out ourselves without the benefit of your wise instincts, Romney.' He paused, looking down at her. 'Romney and Taormina. They don't go together?'

Romney blushed and smiled. 'I suppose even the best of parents, as ours are, can unintentionally cast a blight over their children's lives. Taormina and I are constantly being embarrassed by that question. But we do go together if you understand that approximately nine months before I was born my parents spent a short holiday in and around Rye. By the time they were planning for Taormina four years later, they were able to afford two weeks in Sicily. We always wonder what they'd have called her, had she been a boy!'

'It's a pretty idea, though, commemorating what must have meant a lot to them in their daughters' names.' He turned to watch the antics of a bright yellow aqua-scooter out at sea. 'There goes the speed merchant. Torben has been left way behind. Strange that it doesn't affect him the way a boat does.' He looked down at Romney again. 'So you've no help to give us, Romney?'

'I'm sorry.' Her eyes were warm with regret and she wanted to touch him, but she knew what would happen to her if she did.

'I'm surprised to find you so reticent when you've already worked to considerable good where Kit is concerned, whatever your motives may have been.' He saw her flinch and his eyes hardened as he seemed to remember who and what she was. 'Or is it that you want to keep him in some way dependent on you ... Believing that you're the only person in the world who cares a damn about him?'

She closed her eyes tiredly. 'Do you really believe that?'

There was a short silence and, perplexed, she opened her eyes to find Justin appraising her with an odd twisted expression which slowly became a reluctant smile.

'No. No, I don't. I think I'm beginning to like you much better than I did,' he told her wryly. 'I think you have a natural concupiscence that makes you both improvident and indiscriminate, but I think you also have a finely developed instinct for good and peace. You are a kind girl, and generous ... Aren't you? They used to make songs about women like you.'

'Oh, yes, the tart with the heart of gold,' she agreed bitterly, wondering if he meant to hurt her or simply couldn't help it.

'Except that you don't look the part,' he added musingly, the expression in his eyes made open to doubt by the tinted lenses as he scrutinised her petite slenderness and the pure lines of her calm face, and Romney felt the shocking lurch of desire in her loins once more, knowing he wanted her and able to imagine how it would be with a clarity that made heat steal into her face and body.

'Don't,' she whispered.

He shook his head with a faint smile, as if she were a silly child and he in a tolerant, indulgent mood.

Then the austerity fell on his face again and he asked tautly, 'So just what do I owe my brother, Romney? You tell me not to blame myself, but to a degree, I have to ... How do I recompense him for all that he was deprived of?'

'I don't know,' she responded wearily.

Too much was at stake and the solution was beyond the reach of her limited mind and intuition. The brothers were of a statue she couldn't match, in their personalities, their hatreds and their tragedies. Their lives were made up of drama, hers merely an ordinary life; they understood hatred, she only knew love.

'But you know him.'

'I do know,' she began quietly, her trepidation making her hesitant and unable to look at him. 'I do know that you could still hurt him, that there is something you could do that would hurt him more than anything that has gone before between you.'

'You're referring to yourself, your position in this?' Justin's voice had grown silkily dangerous. 'You're hardly the central issue, sweetheart. I think you're flattering yourself, or else you're overestimating Kit's capacity to love. He's not like our father; he's too selfish to be capable of any great depth of love. It won't hurt him to lose you.'

'Justin, please don't——'

'And I happen to want you,' he added arrogantly. 'Besides which, you and Kit don't suit each other at all. You're kind, he's cruel——'

'And what are you?' she interrupted desperately. 'I think you're plain blind, Justin. You know I'm too weak to withstand ... And if you ... did, it would hurt Kit so badly. Please!'

'It's you who are blind, darling, in this one area at least,' he retorted cuttingly, and laughed as she turned away despairingly. 'Perhaps as you're such a generous lady, Kit and I should share your favours. You'd be satisfied, with all your tastes catered for, and ... Well, what could bring two brothers together more effectively than sharing a woman?'

Her dark hair swung out as she shook her head miserably and began to walk up the beach to the great open-sided building where they were to eat.

They had so far to go still, Justin and Kit, she thought anguishedly, and her presence now, at showdown time, could only drive them even further apart than before. It might be better if she disappeared—except for Kit's need of her.

But to stay! That would be to add immeasurably to the danger. It would make disaster inevitable, because she knew that what Justin had created in her, with so little care and regard, and with so much contempt, was too strong a thing for her to deny alone. She needed his complicity. He must be the one to make the denial, or she would be lost, and Kit lost, and ultimately, Justin lost as well.

And he hadn't even promised to refrain from snorkelling and para-sailing and thus free Kit of the obligation to endure an afternoon's discomfort, she realised unhappily.

Sighing, she sat down at the table at which Helle Elstrom and Otto Adelbert were already ensconced with beers. Helle looked at her sad face with a sympathetic smile but said nothing, but all Otto's deep-rooted instincts towards keeping holiday-makers happy came into play at the sight of her and instead of being able to relax, she was forced to pin a smile on her face and assure him that she was having a marvellous time, because she couldn't bear to disappoint anybody and she really liked Otto, a shy, serious, heavily built man whom she thought of as a light-brown man because that was the colour of his hair, his eyes and, often, his clothes.

'And Pattaya pleases you?' he persisted when he had ordered her a Coke and she had finished rhapsodising about the coral they had seen.

'I love it.' Romney hesitated only slightly as she sensed a presence behind her and knew that Justin had followed her up from the beach. 'It offers everything, the simple life and the glamorous life, side by side.'

'Ah yes, the glamour,' he agreed. 'That is why it has become so popular as a location for fashion-shoots.'

'Yes, there was that French group last month,' she recalled politely.

'And soon we are to have another group from your own country,' he informed her and Justin. 'The photographer is very famous.'

'Titled?' she enquired mischievously.

'No, but one of the models is.'

'Annabel Difford?' Justin guessed, coming round and taking a seat, signalling a waiter.

'Lady Annabel Difford,' Otto corrected precisely.

'I know her well,' Justin replied, his smile warm.

You would, Romney thought with uncharacteristic acidity. And you probably mean intimately.

When the last two members of their party joined them, Kit was in a mood to assert himself, insisting that Romney move down to one end of the table with him, and she complied, not wanting to upset him although isolating themselves in such a manner seemed both juvenile and discourteous.

'I saw you with Justin on the beach,' he accused in an undertone when they were all occupied with their delicious luncheon of crabmeat and other delicacies from the sea. 'What was he saying to you?'

'If you really want to know, he was wondering how much he is to blame for . . . the way you are,' she answered rather shortly.

Kit's expression grew uncertain, vulnerable, and she experienced a pang of remorse.

'Truly, Rom?'

'He loves you, Kit.'

His face hardened once more. 'Don't be a fool. I've told you, he's incapable of that sort of feeling. And it's not his guilt I want! Does he still believe— what he believed this morning?'

'Yes.'

'You won't tell him?'

'You know, Kit, sometimes I look at myself and see the way I comply with your every demand——'

'Not every one,' he cut in significantly.

'The ones that matter. And I think, I'm turning into a doormat! Has it occurred to you that I might be embarrassed by what he thinks?'

'Why? Because, as he suggested, you're ashamed of me?' he taunted.

'Kit.' Romney's eyes and voice were agonised.

'No, sorry, just because you're a nice girl. But you're not a doormat, love. Sometimes you push me around quite unmercifully.' He was wearing his most charming smile and she felt herself softening. 'But indulge me in this. It's a matter of pride. Keep my secret?'

'Yes, all right.'

'And ... the other thing?' His eyes were guarded.

'And the other thing.' She felt the old affection stirring, revivifying, and she touched his hand lovingly, uncaring that Justin watched.

'Has he made a pass yet?' Kit asked abruptly.

She managed a shrug. 'Perhaps at Helle.'

He laughed and she expelled a relieved sigh. That was one of the things she loved most about Kit. He could usually be diverted by an appeal to his sense of humour.

'Never! She'd never let him get in first. I bet she made the first move,' he whispered, and Romney laughed.

'You know, I don't think she ever really does anything. Have you seen the way she looks at her Torben? She's a nice kind lady.' She paused and asked abruptly, 'Kit, who is Annabel Difford?'

'Annabel? Has Justin been talking about her?'

'And Otto. She's due here on a modelling assignment, apparently.'

'She only works part time. But that's great

news.' Kit's smile contained genuine pleasure. 'She's one of the few women Justin has periodically returned to over the years. She's a fantastic person, Romney, and quite amazingly beautiful, even though she must be getting close to the Big Threes ... A really nice lady, and a lady in the true sense of the word. I've always thought that if only Justin would settle down with her, he'd turn into a much nicer person.'

'Why doesn't he?' Romney realised she was holding her breath.

The golden head moved from side to side. 'Scared of commitment—terrified of loving. He saw what it made of our father: a shell.'

'Sometimes, Kit, you're very sensitive,' she said.

'I do understand my brother, Rom. Sometimes,' he added sadly.

After the meal, they left the others and went to look at the market which occupied one side of the great open structure because Kit was a compulsive shopper, and shopping in Thailand allowed him to exercise the full range of his dramatic talents. He looked shocked, he grew offended, then pained, he almost wrung his hands in despair, he turned away dejectedly. The young Thai vendor, fifteen at the most, with whom he was bargaining over a cotton robe, eyed his Longines watch and pronounced it a fake. He would accept it instead of money.

Finally they concluded the deal and Kit paid the price he knew the boy had intended to get all along.

'What about you, Rom?' he asked. 'Do you like that skirt? Shall I buy it for you? It'd suit you.'

It was full-length, of soft brilliant white cotton with a glowing band of embroidery just below knee level, gold with minute flowers in emerald, cerulean blue and cerise.

'No, this would suit her better.'

Justin had joined them and the skirt he was indicating was a deep scarlet, the embroidery also gold, but otherwise there was no other colour on it.

The faint colour in Romney's cheeks grew deeper and her lips were compressed as she glanced up at him, understanding. Kit also understood.

'He thinks you're a scarlet woman, darling!' he exclaimed delightedly. 'We'll have to be more discreet ... Or is it for her royal nature, Jus? But royal purple and deep pink are her colours, because they're warm and womanly and tender ... And white, because she's pure in heart, believe me.'

'If in no other way.' Justin spoke drily.

Romney fingered the scarlet skirt, waiting until she could be sure of controlling her voice. 'It's a better cotton, but ...' She gave Justin a tight-lipped smile. 'I agree with Kit. The white would suit me better.'

Kit bargained for the skirt with less than his customary flair, disappointing the young salesman. It seemed that he was distracted by the distress Romney was endeavouring to conceal.

When the transaction was made, he looked at his brother with his face flushed, but his eyes were steady and resolute.

'Don't insult her any more, Jus,' he requested quietly. 'It's not her fault. She's not to blame for ... us.'

Justin looked at him, then at Romney, a long, considering, clear-eyed look. 'I'm sorry,' he said equally quietly and Romney looked at Kit with loving pride and didn't care who saw it.

Kit's manner changed. 'I suppose you're ready to go snorkelling or whatever,' he ventured with forced cheerfulness, his muscles tensing.

'I thought I'd give it a miss and spend the afternoon in a deck-chair in the shade,' Justin drawled. 'I think I'm suffering from delayed jet-lag, if such a thing is possible.'

Kit's relief was pitiful to see. 'Then I'll join you,' he decided nonchalantly.

Romney let him move ahead. Then she touched Justin's arm, lightly. He looked at her.

'Thank you,' she mouthed silently.

He inclined his head, still looking at her, and his lips stretched into the semblance of a smile, but there was no warmth in the grey eyes, only resignation.

A few minutes later, Helle Elstrom stood with hand on hips, surveying the four men stretched out on loungers or in deck-chairs.

'A typical picture of the modern male!' She grinned at Romney. 'Slothful, indolent, leaving everything, even sports, to the women.'

'But my darling, I thought that was the way you wanted it?' Torben protested. 'The way women have arranged it?'

'Ah, but being a woman, Torben, she naturally wants to both have her cake and eat it.' Justin was surveying both Helle and Romney with lazily narrowed eyes. 'She wants to see us sweating. I wonder if it occurred to anyone at the inception of the sex revolution that one of the most obvious results would be whole generations of emasculated men.'

'Emasculated!' Helle scorned, the wicked laughter in her eyes seeming to suggest that she had personal knowledge to the contrary. 'Although, you know, I might start to believe it if you're going to sit here idle all the afternoon!'

'You ask too much, Helle,' Justin retorted teasingly. 'Having been utterly demoralised by the way women have invaded our territory and taken over our traditional rôles, we are now taking the line of least resistance. We will sit back and become passive observers!'

Only a man totally assured of his own masculine identity could tease like that and betray no trace of resentment, Romney reflected, looking at him. She said in her own gently mocking way:

'So even now men are still better off than women were under the old system. We were never leisurely observers; we were mere obedient, voiceless chattels.'

'And today we occupy two rôles and men none if Justin is serious,' Helle laughed. 'Well, come, Romney, let us show them that we are the stronger sex, with too much energy to waste an afternoon in such idle manner.'

'As long as it's not snorkelling!'

'Para-sailing, I think.' They left the men and strolled on to the hot soft sand, and Helle resumed thoughtfully, 'It is true that we occupy a dual rôle, don't you think, and that makes us still subject to the demands of men, because that is what they expect of us. They demand that we be strong and equal and at the same time they want us in the traditional womanly rôle.'

'They demand altogether too much,' Romney said a little sadly, her mind on Justin and Kit. 'They expect such . . . strength.'

'Ah, but always remember, Romney, that it is because they subconsciously recognise that we are in fact the stronger sex.'

Romney looked sceptical. 'To be strong for one, yes, but for two . . .' she murmured and her voice trailed away hopelessly because she had no right to share the brothers' affairs with Helle, and anyway, to have enabled the older woman to advise her would have meant first breaking the promise Kit had long ago extracted from her.

Helle looked at her knowingly. 'They quarrel over you, the brothers?'

Romney smiled faintly. 'Well, let's say I'm a possible source of conflict.'

'Ach, I know which one I would choose, but perhaps you are the maternal type?' Helle laughed. 'Now, Kit, he makes me think always of my young nephew in Copenhagen. Everyone wants to cuddle him, sit him on their laps, and sometimes he will let them, and be very sweet, but other times he will push them away.'

Small boys the world over, Romney thought ruefully . . . Because that was all Kit was at times, but the burden he bore was too heavy for a child to carry alone without the guidance and support of an adult hand.

A short while later, airborne, free and yet secure in her harness, the brightly coloured parachute filled with air above her, the motor boat like a small toy below, Romney sighed, because her mind was still not free. Even up here, probably the nearest she would ever get to flying, outside of a plane which never really felt like flying, the Faulkner brothers still possessed her. She was still haunted by the intolerable conflicting demands each made on her, setting up her own personal inner conflict, a struggle between desire and kindness, need and duty.

And where on earth was she to find the

strength and the wisdom to subdue the equally insistent demands of her own passionate inclination? Of love she had enough, but not of strength or wisdom, and she would need those in equal measure if she was to make the vital, the crucial, denial.

# CHAPTER FIVE

'SAWATDEE!'

'*Sawatdee,*' Romney replied to the beautiful young Thai girl, a member of the hotel staff, putting her palms together, fingers pointing upward, and dipping her head shyly.

Then they smiled delightedly, pleased with themselves and each other, and Romney moved on round the deep blue swimming-pool to where Kit sprawled on a cushioned lounger in the shade of one of the little thatched cones clustered about the pool.

'Where have you been?' he demanded imperiously as she dropped on to the lounger beside his.

'Down to town to buy a few things,' she replied mildly. 'More suntan lotion, wine to drink with my dinner, some orange squash——'

'Oh, Romney!' Kit relaxed, laughing. 'Why go all the way into town when all those things are available right here at the hotel?'

'But at such outrageous prices, Kit,' she protested seriously, and he laughed again.

'Otto would be horrified if he knew.'

'Lots of guests do it.'

'But you know we can afford the hotel prices, love,' Kit went on.

He could, she thought wryly. It was all his money.

But she only said peaceably, 'I know, but my mother brought me up to be economical. Don't try to change me, Kit.'

She was too sensitive to remind him that the time was coming when she would have to live economically from necessity rather than choice or habit, but perhaps he caught the sad little thought that fluttered through her mind and constricted her heart, because his sapphire eyes grew bleak and brooding.

'And it's my money you're watching so carefully, isn't it?' he taunted bitterly. 'Where's the point, Romney?'

'Kit,' she breathed painfully, making no attempt to conceal the spasm of anguish that crossed her face, because her pain was something he needed to know of.

The bright head was turned towards her and he watched the extra brightness come to her eyes with almost detached interest, but seconds later he was sighing and looking considerably older than his twenty-three years.

'Sorry, love,' he said huskily, putting out a hand to touch her arm.

'Don't keep on testing me, Kit,' she begged, still close to weeping. 'Just accept that I do—love you, and that . . . I will be——'

'Yes, all right, we've got beyond the stage of having to explain ourselves,' he interrupted with a savagely brilliant smile as he stood up swiftly. 'And you, Rom, just accept that I'm a bastard with no consideration for your poor tender feelings . . . Swim with me?'

With a quivering sigh of relief, Romney stood up, discarding the brief tunic that matched one of her tiniest bikinis, mere scraps of thin white quick-drying fabric scattered with bright saffron flowers.

Kit never really swam. He merely frolicked about, seldom going out of his depth, and Romney was content to do likewise, grateful for his change of mood after the sullen resentment which had characterised his dealings with everyone over the last two days, ever since their return by launch from the Gulf's islands when he had been unable to conceal the fact of his sea-sickness and had interpreted a smile from Justin as cynically disparaging. Deep in the back of her mind, Romney knew that his present cheerfulness was forced, either for her sake or for reasons of his own, but just for now she weakly succumbed to the temptation to relax, pretending it was real, pretending there was no shadow . . .

'Incidentally,' he laughed up at her when she had hauled herself out of the pool to sit with her slim legs dangling in the water. 'You won't be needing to use any of your wine tonight. We've got a date.'

She looked down at him with the familiar softening sensation in the region of her heart and a tightness in her throat. When he smiled like that, with pleasure and affection and a trace of mischief, he was truly beautiful, a perfect young god, all golden in the sunshine. He reminded her of a puppy or, rather, a kitten, because however open he was, he had that feline quality of still keeping part of himself in reserve. Kit might love her, but he kept his secrets.

'What are we doing?' she asked happily, too human not to appreciate the lifestyle Kit had made available to her although the price she paid for it was higher than she could have guessed when she had made her promises to him a year ago.

'What do you say to the Tiffany Show and a meal somewhere along the waterfront?' The brilliant eyes were narrow with humour. 'I can't wait to see Justin suffering the same sort of sexual identity crisis that hit me the first time we saw it. Remember the one who did Evita, Rom?'

'Is Justin going?'

Romney's face had closed. Ever since their day out in the Gulf, she had endeavoured to avoid Justin Faulkner, for all their sakes. It had not been easy. Kit wanted to be with his brother, in his company, and yet he refused to be alone with him, continually demanding Romney's protection, as if he feared that his brother might somehow break him, or break him down and extract his last appalling secret. So, she had hovered quietly but faithfully on the sidelines of their wary, hostile encounters, always ready to rescue the younger brother, always frightened of the older.

'It was his idea.'

With the rash courage of desperation, she decided on candour and the risk of an explosion from Kit.

'Kit? Wouldn't it be better, wouldn't you stand a chance of some sort of a reconciliation if the two of you could be alone together without my presence to inhibit you?'

'Oh, Rom, I know you mean well and for my sake . . .' His eyes avoided hers and he glanced away to the end of the pool before bending the burnished head that had remained dry, and kissing her knee. 'Anyway, I don't fancy playing gooseberry to him and Annabel.'

'Annabel?' She laid a hand on his bare shoulder in the automatic, slack caress of passionless love.

'She arrived this morning.' He looked up at her again and he was wearing his Faun's face. 'It was edifying to witness. She and Justin got together with all the relief of former lovers who find themselves together with no better prospect in sight.'

With an oddly colourless feeling, as if all emotion and all hope had suddenly drained away from her, Romney looked down at the golden head before turning her gaze towards the end of the pool. Her pulses leapt, and then settled dully as she understood what Kit had been about.

'Oh, Kit, did you need to confirm it for him?' she sighed with the merest vestige of sarcasm. 'He was in no doubt, you know.'

Kit went on smiling at her, not denying the resigned charge, but the blue eyes hardened as they rested on her vulnerable face.

'As long as you don't cause him to doubt it,' he warned, very softly. 'Remember that, my love.'

The sun was on her head and shoulders, the lukewarm water about her legs, but she only felt the chill that spread through her as she comprehended his threat. Silently she swung her legs out of the water and stood up shakily, while Kit waded towards the steps, waving in welcome to Justin and the slender woman who stood at his side as if she belonged there by right.

They returned to their own patch of shade and Kit drew up an extra lounger and a chair as the other couple came to join them.

Romney looked at Annabel Difford and wondered why Kit had worried. With such a creature at his side, Justin would hardly look at another woman. She was walking, talking perfection, all grace and glow. Older than most models still working, the extra years merely seemed to have added a lustre, made her a whole, complete woman instead of a clothes rack. Her hair was a rippling mass of dark, dark red, like an old-fashioned red-black rose, her eyes shadowy green and filled with mystery, her complexion cream and palest pink. She was all simple enchantment and yet she also radiated an aura of age-old feminine mystique.

'Romney,' she said with genuine pleasure when Justin had introduced them and ordered three Mai Tais and a coke for Kit. 'Justin has been telling me how you came to be named and I think it's just so incredibly romantic. I've decided that when I have my children, I'm going to make sure they're conceived in lovely, lovely places and do the same.'

She meant it too. There could be no doubting her warmth and sincerity. Beautiful looks and a beautiful nature. Romney should have been relieved because surely such a woman must turn Justin aside from his expressed intention of taking her away from Kit—but she only felt the beginning of despair, like the blackened edges of a frosted flower starting to curl up and die.

Beside Annabel, so sparkling and exquisite, she felt dumbly ineloquent, and ordinary, plain— earthbound—while Annabel was surely made in some realm beyond the world's prosaic system and sent here to exacerbate the eternally frustrated desire for perfection that was the curse of mortals, by showing them what they would never achieve.

'Gorgeous Annabel,' Kit was purring outrageously, with a wicked glance at Justin. 'Did you know that you arrived in the nick of time to save Justin from the frolicsome attention of a gambolling Great Dane?'

'I've met her and I think your observation is both cruel and unjust, dear Kit,' Annabel returned, but smilingly, and Romney went on watching her as she and Kit began a friendly argument about Helle Elstrom.

Annabel's figure was perfect too, and revealed to alluring advantage by the diminutive sea-green bikini. Her perfection brought a bitter knowledge to Romney. She realised that having known a woman like Annabel, and probably others just as gorgeous, Justin Faulkner's apparent desire for her could hardly have been aroused by any merits she herself might possess. She couldn't begin to compete with a woman like Annabel. She had to face it. The fact that she was Kit's girlfriend was what had made her attractive in Justin's eyes. As twisted as his brother, he was motivated by some sadistic urge to hurt Kit, to punish him for the years behind, just as Kit was equally anxious to find some way of inflicting hurt on Justin.

She looked at Justin and found him watching her, cruel amusement lightening the grey eyes. She felt her heart slow painfully and then pick up speed, beginning to race, and breathing became difficult. There was that twisting, strangling sensation within her and a dryness to her mouth as she stared helplessly at him, unable to tear her gaze away from the austerely beautiful face and the vibrant masculinity of his body, the smooth hard flesh much darker now than it had been a few days ago, just as the ash fair hair was lighter. He wore only his dark swimming trunks and, seeing him like that, Romney felt her imagination stir and wake, pushing out all other considerations. It was the imagination of the senses, all her senses, because she seemed to know exactly how it would be, to be close to that magnificent body, joined to it. She thought she knew the taste and scent of him, just as she knew the sight and sound, and the awareness that such knowledge could never be reality was unbearable in that moment, tearing her apart so that she drew a quick gasping breath of pain before managing to withdraw her eyes with an effort of will that brought further pain.

She glanced anxiously at Kit to reassure herself that he had not witnessed her moments of weakness; and then at Annabel Difford for the strengthening reminder that, having known such a woman, Justin couldn't possibly want her for any qualities of her own but merely because possessing her would hurt Kit.

'Don't feel too safe.' Justin had drawn his chair close to the side of her lounger and he spoke in a voice too low for the others to hear, head bent towards her, and the silken note reminded her strangely of Kit when he made threats.

'Safe?' But she knew he had read her thoughts.

He smiled slowly. 'Annabel is part of the past. You are the present, Romney.'

Romney's face was a still, frozen mask of desperation. 'Don't, Justin,' she whispered urgently.

'Why not?' he taunted softly. 'You want me, don't you? And I could have you so very easily . . .'

She bowed her dark head in acknowledgement but when she looked up at him again, her sherry-coloured eyes held the sparkle of a bitter knowledge.

'And Kit would never forgive you, and I would never forgive you.' She paused and when she resumed, her voice had sunk to a breathless, horrified murmur as she grasped the full measure of the disaster he meant to bring about. 'And ultimately, Justin, you would never forgive yourself.'

'How dramatic you make it all sound,' he drawled.

'Oh, believe me, believe me!' she entreated while agony lanced through her.

'Tell me why I should?' he invited easily.

But that was just what she couldn't do, held by a promise she had made, one that meant so very much to Kit.

'You just don't give a damn about your brother, do you?' she accused in an angry, unhappy mutter.

'He's less sensitive than you think, Romney. He could stand to lose you,' Justin assured her caustically.

'You're the one who is insensitive!'

Appalled by his callousness, she turned her head away to look at Kit, failing to notice the impatience that suddenly tightened Justin's face. Kit was still chattering amicably to an indulgent Annabel, but Romney saw that he was squinting slightly in the brilliance of the reflected sunlight that came up off the pool water. She sat up and reached for the sunglasses lying on the table, and leaned forward to touch Kit's arm.

'Put them on,' she said quietly and he took them from her with a grateful smile.

'For God's sake!' The wildly irritated explosion came from Justin, shocking them all, and Romney paled as she realised that his anger was directed at her. 'Must you always carry on as though you were his mother and he a damned baby? I suppose you also tell him to wash behind his ears and remind him to brush his teeth at bedtime? I'm surprised you let him into the pool without water-wings ... He's a big boy now, Romney! You know ... You should know,' he added significantly.

Kit too had turned white, but now his face was

scarlet as he sprang up, trembling with the fury
Romney knew and feared.

'What do you know about it, Justin?' he
demanded petulantly. 'Perhaps that's what I like,
perhaps I enjoy having someone like Romney to
. . . to mother me! After all, I never knew my own
mother, did I? You and the old bore at home think
yourselves so hard-done-by, but you were better
off than me . . . You at least knew her for some
years. That's never occurred to you in all the years
you've been blaming me, has it?'

'How wrong can a man be?' Justin taunted, eyes
glittering contemptuously. 'After all, it seems, you
are very immature and perhaps you do still need a
maternal influence in your life . . . I'm just
surprised you don't go in for older women instead
of babies like Romney.'

Kit who seemed to pause, temper abating as he
looked from Romney to Annabel who was
tactfully pretending a deep interest in the antics of
some children in the pool. Romney could see the
wicked glint forming in his eyes and read the
outrageous idea in the moment it occurred to him.
It was hovering on his lips already and it would
embarrass her and insult Annabel—

Turning swiftly to Justin, she said reproachfully,
'Why did you ignore your opportunity? Tell him!'

'He's not worth the effort, Romney!' He was
beginning to sound bored. 'And I don't know why
you take so much trouble on his behalf either.'

'Tell him you don't still blame him,' she insisted,
exasperated.

'Leave it, Rom.' Kit was looking embarrassed.

'No, she's right, Kit,' Justin changed his mind
suddenly—probably just to be contrary, Romney
suspected. 'Let's at least get that out of the way.

I'm sure you'll still find ample reason for hating me, without that. Understand that I do not and have not, since you were a very small boy, blamed you or resented you for anything—anything at all, Kit. I'm just sorry that I was once young enough to be influenced by our father whose loss made him blind to reason.'

'Forget it, Jus.' Kit was suddenly shy, yet his response was gracious and mature, and Romney felt proud of him. 'I realise with hindsight that you tried to make amends, and I . . . Well, I was also once too young to see things clearly.'

Justin nodded curtly and Romney was swept by a wave of relief although she knew the reconciliation, if it could even be called that, fell far short of what Kit secretly hoped for. Nevertheless, it was something, a small concession on both their parts, and something of a miracle when one knew of the wilful blindness of both brothers.

She got up and went to sit on the edge of the pool, and after a minute Annabel Difford joined her. They exchanged wryly amused sidelong glances.

'Always April weather,' Annabel commented. 'They've always been like that. But you're a better woman than I, Romney Channer. I could never stir myself to act as a peacemaker in that particular conflict.'

'I hardly think peace is what has been made,' Romney confided ruefully.

'No. Sometimes I think hostility has become a habit with them, and yet I know it worries Justin, although he won't admit it.'

She glanced back at Justin and Romney saw the green eyes grow tender and knew that Annabel loved Justin and had done for a long time. And

Justin—Justin was incapable of loving, his father's love for his mother having bred in him a morbid fear of that emotion.

Shadow lay on them all, she reflected, and knew that she had never understood despair until now, because it seemed impossible that the shadow would ever lift for all of them. It was an effort to remind herself that some people managed to achieve happiness, but the sight of the Elstroms cavorting in the deep end helped her and she was able to look at Annabel with a smile.

'It worries Kit too,' she said.

'Romney, is he unwell?' Annabel asked abruptly.

'No! No,' she repeated more calmly. 'He suffers from occasional headaches, that's all ... That's why I wanted him to put on his sunglasses.'

'And thereby triggered off quite a little drama,' Annabel laughed reminiscently and Romney relaxed.

She swam again, and Annabel joined her, staying in when Romney finally got out.

Justin and Kit were still in the shade, silent as they occupied themselves with their drinks, she saw with regret. Becoming aware of her approach, they both looked up and watched her, and it was the sensual appraisal of light silvery-grey eyes that caused the deep burning flush to spread over her skin, Romney knew. The younger man's sapphire eyes, hidden behind dark lenses now, could never affect her thus, however much she loved him.

It was Kit who stood up, laying an arm across her shoulders, and for once Romney took comfort and strength from him instead of the other way round, turning in to him and leaning, sensing the faint frisson of surprised pleasure that ran through him as she did so.

He smiled his most scintillating smile at the older brother who watched them with a cynical curve to his lips.

'Romney isn't just a ... a mother to me, Justin, you know,' Kit claimed with charming deprecation. 'She's everything, whatever I need her to be, whenever I need her, and there's a private side to our life together ... I'm sure you'll understand and excuse us if we desert you. I think we need to be alone. Here's your tunic, my love. See you later, Jus.'

Romney let him walk her away, relaxing once she no longer had to withstand the laser quality of Justin's gaze and no longer needing the comfort of physical contact with Kit, especially when it was so hot, but she was feeling pleased with him, and so she let him keep his arm about her as they walked towards their rooms.

'Come in and raid my mini-bar,' he invited at his door. 'Since I took you away before you'd finished your Mai Tai. Water for me, though.'

Romney sat and sipped her gin-and-tonic on the bougainvillaea-decked balcony overlooking the sultry Gulf of Siam, viewing Kit's new tranquillity with pleasure. He seemed, almost, serene.

'You're feeling happier, aren't you?'

'Yes,' he agreed softly. 'Now he's said it, though I've known it for years. Thank you. It was your doing.'

Her smile grew mischievous. 'I had to say something. That was a terrible suggestion you were going to make about Annabel and me. I could see it forming in your mind.'

'You always could read my thoughts,' he agreed ruefully. 'But I'm glad you intervened, love. Both you and Lady Annabel deserve better. All the

same, I'd love to have seen Justin's face had I
actually come out with it.'

'Why? Do you think he secretly does love
Annabel but won't admit it?' Romney was aware
of having stiffened and she felt guilty, because
Annabel deserved to have her love reciprocated.

'You're not being very bright, my darling,' Kit
reproached sarcastically. 'No, what I think is that
my usually impervious big brother seems a trifle
resentful of your devotion to me.'

Romney put down her glass and looked at him
with dawning comprehension. 'And that's what
you want, isn't it?' she challenged flatly, her
expression growing resigned as she realised that
not one but both brothers were attempting to use
her as a pawn in the deadly contest between them.
'You want Justin to . . . to——'

'To want you.' Kit was looking pleased with
himself. 'That's it, exactly. Just as long as you
don't actually let him—have you. I'm a little
worried, though, by the fact that you're so very . . .
human, my dearest Rom.'

'It's you I love,' she protested automatically.

'Oh, love,' he disparaged. 'Love and Justin are
scarcely synonymous. I was talking about sex.'

'You're both the same,' Romney accused
bitterly. 'You both manipulate people.'

'Don't be cross,' he begged, wearing his most
angelic expression. 'Try to understand. Just once,
just for once, I want him to envy something I
have. All my life I've had to watch him excelling at
things and then know myself a failure at the same
things. He's acknowledged as a genius in the
commercial world, he swims better and faster than
I do, he doesn't get sick on the sea . . . And he
attracts women who are not only beautiful, but

nice, Romney. Women who are really too good for him because they all love him and he only uses them ... Apart from you, the girls I've attracted have all been rather ... silly, to put it as kindly as possible.'

'All human beings are silly when they fall in love,' she reflected absently. 'But, Kit, you're a different person from Justin. You're good at different things. You're creative. You can paint and draw, and write poetry, and you act like a dream ... I don't know why you ever gave that up.'

'I suppose, because I suspected that he and my father didn't really respect it as a career,' Kit ventured rather sulkily.

'I don't know your father.' Romney hesitated. 'But Justin is a highly intelligent man, Kit. He must be aware of how difficult and demanding a career acting is.'

Kit shrugged. 'Well anyway, I did give it up and it's too late to do anything about it now. I was always restless anyway. I think I always sensed ... Oh, well!' He drank some water and smiled with another of his mercurial changes of mood. 'Anyway, the point is, it would be very nice, and gratifying, to see Justin jealous of me for a change. And you are the instrument.'

'Oh, Kit.' She laughed faintly. 'When he has known a woman like Annabel Difford?'

'Don't you know how very special you are, Romney?' His smile grew loving. 'The only reason I haven't tried harder to ... ah, to ravish you, is because I love you so much, and Otto Adelbert would propose marriage tomorrow if he wasn't so honourable and didn't think I had a prior claim.'

'Kit.' Romney spoke very quietly. 'What about my feelings?'

He looked contrite, but resolute. 'Oh, angel, I know! But . . .' His most charming smile flashed out. 'But you love me, don't you?'

Had he been any other young man or even Kit Faulkner but undoomed, his end unknown, she would have walked out. But she shared his secret.

'Of course.' She stood up, holding her drink. 'But, let me be . . . alone for a while. I'll see you when it's time to leave for town.'

When he smiled so gently and sadly, she knew she could deny him nothing.

But in the blessed privacy of her own suite, she thought wildly—they'll destroy me!

Between them, the brothers would destroy her. She had no defence, because they possessed her utterly, like both the daemons of nightmare and the angels of sweet, sustaining dreaming. She was beyond hope of liberty, bound to them irrevocably, because she could never know bonds stronger than those of love and compassion.

Sometimes Romney wondered where she found the strength to endure, but in her more analytical moments, she knew that it wasn't strength but loving that sustained her.

When the time came to leave for town, she took her place at Kit's side as calmly as if there had never been a moment's doubt or dilemma.

Kit was in a mood to shock. 'Did you know there are something like one hundred V.D. clinics in Pattaya?' he demanded on the way down in their open-backed taxi.

Romney pointedly changed the subject before anyone could respond, talking valiantly about the Thai royals and the people's pride in their country's system, their love for king, queen and prince. Annabel Difford responded gallantly but the men only smiled with indulgence or cynicism, and Romney wondered unhappily how the evening would end. Men could be so unco-operative!

But when it came to the Tiffany Show, she could feel almost encouraged. For Annabel and herself, it was merely a curiosity, the fact that the Evita, the Marilyn and the Bassey were biological males, but for Justin and Kit it was a matter for serious discussion.

After the show, they went to one of the waterfront restaurants, dining outside, watching the lights on the water. The setting was functional, the tables bare, but such places were an essential part of the Pattaya experience and the food was as good as any in the world. They all opted for prawns, making their own selection and watching them being prepared, and Justin ordered himself a half-bottle of French wine while Romney and Annabel shared a delicate Australian white.

The men were still talking about the show and related issues and Romney watched them and thought—I love them both. In such very different ways, though.

Kit was relating a startling experience he had had at a nightclub in Bangkok's *Patpong* road when he had ventured there alone soon after their arrival in Thailand.

Romney knew the story so she gave herself up to the pleasure of watching Justin. His clear grey eyes were alight with interest and amusement as they rested on his brother's mobile face, and his mouth had become beautiful once more with that smile playing about it and occasionally becoming laughter.

She had known from the beginning that she loved him; had known from her own response to him because she knew herself and knew consequently that nothing else but love could have aroused her to such a pitch. But now it was as if she made the discovery afresh, because the frail damming with which she had tried to contain the emotion had given way before the growth and strengthening and increase of her love.

Love surged and rushed through her, overwhelming her, and with it came fear for Justin because he could not know the grave magnitude of what he intended, and she could not tell him. It was all she could do not to cry a warning then and there, because once he knew the truth, as inevitably he must one day soon, he would find it hard to forgive himself. She knew, with the insight of love, that he was a man who would judge himself very harshly.

Her agony was all for him in that moment, with none for herself and Kit, and she had no idea as she continued utterly absorbed in making love to him with her eyes that Annabel Difford was watching her with painful comprehension.

'Honestly, Justin, I never had an inkling until I touched her and realised something felt wrong,' Kit was concluding his tale. 'I felt such a fool when I asked the other girl, the real one, and she told me—a real innocent abroad! I just slunk out of there with the real girls all giggling away at the *farang*'s embarrassment. Talk about knowing a woman when you see one! I didn't know what wasn't a woman until I touched her . . . or him! I'll never trust my eyes again!'

Justin laughed. 'Now I always know a woman when I . . . sense one.'

The grey eyes came to rest on Romney. Almost crystalline they seemed, filled with light rather than colour, a brilliant softly blazing light, and she was aware of Kit's small secretive smile of satisfaction because what he wanted seemed to be happening.

She trembled and the faint colour in her cheeks grew deeper as she felt the hot lurch of desire in her loins. She was aware of Annabel saying something, to Kit, she thought, but she couldn't attend to it while Justin went on appraising her in that openly sensual way, caressing her with his eyes, touching every part of her, and a purely selfconscious and very feminine part of her was glad she was looking her best tonight. Her dark brown hair was a smooth, sleek bell, her eyes rimmed with kohl, the lashes laden with mascara, and she wore a traditional fine-ply Thai silk outfit of long slim skirt and little jacket with three-quarter length sleeves. She had thought she looked attractive; she had little awareness of an erotic aspect to her appearance, something that lay in the tender, passionate curve of her mouth, the languor of her movements in the hot night air, and the way she looked back at him without the least flutter of her eyelashes to add a coy missish effect, and her visible sensuality was enhanced by the colour of the silk that hid so much of her flesh and thus made temptation stronger. It was a deep magenta, a colour she might have hesitated to wear at home, but in the sultry, seductive East it seemed appropriate.

Justin smiled, a cruel smile, and Romney knew as clearly as if he had told her that he was contemplating the removal of the silk and the long, slow discovery of the flesh beneath that would follow.

And it must not happen, she thought anguishedly, wrenching her gaze away and hating herself for the traitorous melting sensation that was assailing her, and the weak quivering of thighs that longed for the hardness of his.

Kit must tell him the truth, she decided desperately. Somehow she had to persuade Kit to tell him.

# CHAPTER SIX

'KIT?'

They were strolling through the town, about a block ahead of Justin and Annabel, and Kit had stopped to look into one of the open-fronted bazaars.

'Um? Is there anything you fancy here?' He was eager to bargain.

The town was more alive by night than by day, with throngs of people crowding the pavements. Shops, bars and discos were all open, packed with young people, mostly Thais, and the 'butterflies' were out as well. A combination of noise and heat and light made it an exciting place, but Romney was preoccupied.

'No, I don't think so,' she said, not really looking. 'Kit, please, won't you tell Justin the truth?'

'No!'

'Or let me?' she hurried on, already knowing it was futile.

His face was flushed, his mouth twisted into an ugly shape, and his eyes blazed with the rage that came from fear as he clutched at her forearm with cruelly vicious fingers.

'I said no!' he hissed. 'And I'll break your neck if you tell him, Romney.'

'But it's not fair to him to leave him in ignorance,' she pleaded, wincing with pain as his hold on her grew even tighter.

'So, I'm being fair to myself for a change,' he retorted sharply.

'But if he——' She stopped. Justin and Annabel were closing the gap between them and this wasn't an exchange that could bear witnesses.

'Yes? If he—what?' Kit taunted. 'If he tries to seduce you? But why are you worrying? Because he's not going to succeed, is he? You're going to be faithful to me, because I'm the one you love, or so you keep telling me. All I'm asking you to do is prove it.'

'Kit . . .' she breathed protestingly, and her pain was both physical and emotional.

'Promise me,' Kit insisted, his hand sliding down to her wrist and twisting until she made a little moaning sound, convinced that he must break the fragile bones.

'Yes, all right, I promise,' she whispered, torn with pity for the torment she saw behind his anger.

He released her wrist as Justin and Annabel joined them and Romney saw that Justin's mouth was grimly compressed. His eyes went deliberately to the wrist she was nursing in her other hand and, following his gaze, she flushed on seeing the long red marks left on her forearm and wrist by Kit's fingers. When their eyes met again, Justin's were coldly contemptuous.

'I think it's time we were getting back to the hotel,' he said. 'Annabel has an early start tomorrow.'

'Let's take an open taxi again,' Kit suggested, calm and smiling once more. 'It's like a cauldron down here and that way we can cool off in the breeze.'

'Some of us need it,' Justin agreed enigmatically, but for once Kit missed the sardonic inflection.

During the drive back to the hotel, Romney sat

silent and unhappy, wondering where the solution lay. Not in herself, that was for sure, because she just didn't have the strength. If only she could go away and leave the brothers to fight it out between them, without her own presence as an extra area of conflict. But Kit would never agree to that, he needed her too much, and a unilateral decision to depart was practically impossible since she lacked the fare back to England and Kit had all the money. She supposed she could get an unpaid job and shelter and sustenance at one of the refugee camps that were such a burden to Thailand, but she had no idea what qualifications were required and, anyway, once again she came back to Kit's very real need of her and her promise to him.

'Coffee?' Justin suggested when they reached the hotel.

Annabel, who had been quite subdued during the latter part of the evening, murmured something about the famous photographer murdering her if she had bags under her eyes in the morning.

Kit smiled sweetly at them all. 'Then I'll walk you to your room, Annabel. I gave up coffee along with liquor.' He turned to the other two. 'You stay, though, Rom. You'll see her safely to her room, won't you, Justin?'

'But——' Romney began.

'It's all right, love,' Kit insisted gently, wearing his satyr's smile. 'You know how much you enjoy the coffee they do here.'

And Justin's hand was closing gently but firmly round her upper arm, scorching her through the magenta silk and rendering her incapable of any further protest.

'He's making it very easy for me,' Justin commented drily when they were seated at a table in the coffee shop. 'Doesn't he realise I'm going to take you away from him?'

'Perhaps he knows and is giving you the opportunity to try,' Romney ventured tartly because, somehow, she had to warn him, give him some hint.

'Generous of him, but it doesn't show much regard for you.'

'To try and to fail, Justin,' she added pointedly. 'Kit trusts me to be faithful to him.'

'Then he's a fool, because you're not going to be, are you?' The grey eyes glittered with cold derision as he regarded her. 'You're incapable of fidelity, wanting me as you do.'

'You're so arrogant,' she claimed with a touch of wonder.

'No, merely realistic,' he contradicted her lightly. 'The more men, the better, where your appetites are concerned, Romney. Well, we know what they say about variety, and hopefully I'll be able to provide a new experience in the way of sensation.'

Romney felt the warmth unfurling in the base of her stomach once more and her cheeks grew hot.

'Don't!' she begged shakily, her eyes huge and feverish in her gentle face where strain was beginning to show.

Justin merely gave a hard little laugh, sitting back as the waiter arrived with their coffee.

He watched her in silence as she sipped her coffee, so intently that Romney grew self-conscious after a while and set down her cup. Justin smiled.

'And this sort of thing, Romney?' He picked up her hand and looked down at her wrist. The marks on her arm had faded but a light purplish band ran all the way round her narrow wrist. 'Do you enjoy it? Do you get a thrill out of my brother's brutality? I wouldn't have taken you for a masochist.'

'I'm not . . .' She could have freed her hand with very little effort; he was exerting no pressure; but she was beyond all movement save for the curling of her fingers in response to the dry warmth of his hand.

'Then why endure it? Where's your pride?' He swept her face with a hard glance. 'Leave him, Romney.'

'You know nothing about my relationship with Kit,' she told him in a tight little voice. 'And you know nothing about Kit either, if you can want to hurt him in this way.'

'I'm not really doing this to get at Kit. I'm not that childish and I wouldn't insult you like that.' He smiled rather wryly. 'I'm doing it because I happen to want you, rather badly, and because you've made it very clear that you want me. If you didn't, I'd accept it, Romney.'

'Then, all right, I don't want you,' she lied in a numb, stifled tone.

'Liar.' He lifted her hand and pressed his mouth to the discoloured area of her wrist, gently sucking at her skin as if he would draw the pain out of her, and Romney sat absolutely still, mesmerised, although inwardly she knew a wild fluttering sensation that changed to quivering and finally to deep tremors as she felt the hot slide of his tongue delicately stroking over the area. Justin looked at her again, into her, his slow, deliberate smile telling her he knew what she was feeling. 'Our lovemaking will be very much to our mutual delight, won't it? Yours as well as mine.'

He released her hand and picked up his coffee, obviously expecting no reply. They finished drinking at the same time and sat in silence for a full minute. Justin's eyes seemed to darken and burn as he looked at Romney, growing heavy-lidded, and she felt an answering languor in herself.

'Tonight, I think, Romney?' His voice seemed to have thickened.

'No.' Her own was husky.

He merely looked at her and signalled for their bill, and Romney went on gazing at him as he dealt with it. Incredibly, it was beginning to seem as if he really did want her. How such a miracle might have occurred, when he could have women like Annabel Difford, she couldn't imagine, but she supposed there must be something in her that appealed to something in him.

Perhaps human beings were designed in such a way that wanting must be mutual, a chemical thing—only, in her, it was more than wanting; it was loving too.

And desire wasn't love. Nevertheless, to have won even that from him was—oh, incredible. Yet she could hardly find it gratifying because his genuinely wanting her would make it that much harder for her to resist him. Wanting could become need, and then how should she deny him?

It had been easier and she had had some defence while she had believed that he sought merely to punish Kit through her, because then his motives had seemed contemptible. Now, she had nothing save her awareness of Kit's dependence on her loyalty and the bitter knowledge that wanting and needing were not the same thing as loving. She must never forget those things. They must serve now as her talismans.

'Your room is next to Kit's, isn't it?' Justin said as they left the coffee shop.

'There's no need——'

'Kit asked me to, remember,' he interrupted smoothly.

For once the walk seemed too short. Her heart was thudding, breathing was an agony, her legs barely supported her—and, dear God, what was she going to say?

'Good night, Justin,' was all she could think of as she slotted the key into the lock.

'You know I'm coming in with you.'

He moved her gently aside, turning the key and opening the door, reaching round to find the light switch.

'Justin, I can't! We can't!' She looked at him as he turned from closing the door and saw the imperative male demand in his eyes.

She went into his arms with a small despairing sigh. It seemed so long, so long, since there had been anyone stronger than she—a whole lonely, aching year since she had been able to lean on a strength greater than hers, and now there were steely arms about her and a hard body to rest against.

'It's all right, Romney.' Justin's voice was soft and rough as his hands moved to cup her face and he looked down into her eyes. 'You can't help the demands of your blood ... These rooms are perfectly soundproof, but if you feel uncomfortable with Kit next door, we can move to mine?'

'No!' She swallowed convulsively. 'But—Kit! Justin, try to understand——'

'He's not worthy of you, Romney,' he cut in tautly. 'I don't know what you're doing with him. There must be a hundred other, better men you could have ... Only, you love him. I do know that. But, sweet, he doesn't have to know. I want you badly enough to accept your terms. He needn't know.'

She wanted to go on protesting, resisting, but his lips were touching hers, parting them, and his fingers were moving in her hair, sensitising her scalp. Helpless, she slid her arms about him, her long lashes sinking to her cheeks, hiding the agony and guilt in her eyes.

Then Justin's mouth claimed hers, and Kit, and every other consideration slipped away from her.

This was where she belonged, and what she existed for. She shuddered in his arms and felt him tremble in response. He murmured something into her mouth and then his kiss deepened, becoming more intimate, and Romney arched against him involuntarily, impatient to experience all that his kiss promised.

Justin groaned, sharply, and Romney's arms glided up his body until her fingers could tangle in his fair hair, bringing his face closer to hers, deepening their long feverish kiss still further.

It was so personal, so intense, she could almost believe that he felt as she did, and pride and principle no longer mattered.

'Justin!' Her voice was sharp, quivering with the ache of desire as the kiss came to an end.

'I know, darling.' Justin spoke heavily, the words slurred. 'I've never wanted any woman as much as you. Ah, Romney... Always dress this way for me. It makes both the anticipation and the discovery so much sweeter than the obviousness of a bikini.'

His hands shook as he unbuttoned the little magenta jacket and Romney felt perspiration break out, all over her, on her brow and upper lip, between and below her breasts, and at her loins.

She couldn't think, she could only feel. There was no denial she could make. She could only let Justin sweep her down and down, into a dark, golden vortex of desire, hot and honey-sweet.

Her jacket was discarded and the straight narrow skirt followed, slithering to the floor when he had eased it over her hips. He bent to remove her low-heeled soft leather sandals, his long fingers lingering sensitively about the smooth curves of her small feet. Then he straightened and looked at what he had revealed, the slender young body all smooth, creamy golden-brown, its most intimate secrets still kept from him by the little white bra and cool white silk cami-knickers.

She had once thought of Justin as a cold man. Now she saw his eyes darken and grow hotly molten with an intensity of desire that unnerved her a little because she had not anticipated that he could want her to such an extent. But her lower lip felt full and was still throbbing exquisitely from his kiss, and in the next moment fear fled as her own hunger leapt to match his, piercing her with a bittersweet agony. She swayed towards him and he caught her in his arms.

'Kiss me again,' she whispered, her cheeks hot as her head fell back against his arm.

'Romney!' Her name seemed wrung from him and he bent his head to invade the moist sweetness of her mouth once more, drawing her down into a dark torrid sea of swirling sensation. Great waves of passion broke over them, beating at them, robbing them of all control as they clung wildly to each other, gasping as their mouths broke apart and instantly, desperately sought each other again.

Romney's fingers shook violently as she undid the buttons of Justin's pale shirt and loosed it from the belt of his pants, and she murmured incoherently as she found the flesh she sought, sliding her arms round his back, her hands feverishly caressing the smooth muscled flesh.

'Yes!' Justin's voice throbbed with its freight of intolerable desire and she pressed her hot face into the soft fair hair that curled damply on his chest, drawing a sobbing breath as her mouth found the hard male nipple, the spasm that knifed through him telling her that she was stoking his passion still further, instinct telling her of what he required.

Her mouth moved all over his chest and shoulders then, and his neck and throat, in a tantalising journey of erotic little kisses until she drew from him a sound she had not heard from a man before, a long hard male moaning.

He drew back as if he feared for his sanity, his face a taut, tortured mask as he removed his shirt completely.

'How can you be so young and so ... skilled?' he asked raggedly. 'Kit can't have been your first lover as I once thought. How old were you, Romney?'

Kit! She closed her eyes briefly, but before she could summon the voice to protest, Justin was touching her again, steering her gently towards the bed which the room-staff had turned down earlier. With his hands on her, Romney was lost once more, allowing him to push her back on to the soft mattress and swiftly remove her last remaining garments.

'You're beautiful, so very beautiful, and I want to make love to you in every way there is,' Justin

claimed hoarsely, surveying the glowing loveliness
of her taut, damp body. 'But first . . . Tell me what
you want, Romney? What do you like?'

His assumption that she was sufficiently experienced to have tastes and preferences touched her
like an electric shock. Kit was responsible for his
belief—Kit, who lay behind that wall, sleeping or
scheming or enduring the hell of one of his
headaches.

'Justin!' She put a hand up to his shoulder as he
bent over her. 'I think we must . . . stop, now. I
can't . . . I'm sorry . . . Kit trusts me. I can't
betray . . .'

The grey eyes blazed momentarily, but the brief
flare of rage swiftly subsided to an intense
smoulder and he smiled, cruelly.

'I'll stop, Romney, if you can assure me, quite
honestly, that you don't want this.' He covered
one love-swollen breast with his hand and she
drew a shuddering breath, mute as he scrutinised
the hectic colour staining her cheeks and the
feverish glitter of her eyes. 'And this . . .'

His fingers trailed downward to the dark
mystery at her thighs and a long low cry came
from Romney as she quivered jerkily at the shock
of such intimate contact. Justin smiled again, the
smile of a victor.

He began to stroke her, so gently that she
thought she would go out of her mind with the
sweet ecstasy that was almost agony. Desire had
become pain as well as pleasure now. There was a
hollow ache deep inside her, beginning to pulse,
slow heavy beats at first, soon becoming frantic,
like the urgent summons of drums.

'Justin! My darling!' It was a hoarse throbbing
cry, born of her exquisite need for fulfilment, a

plea for him to soothe the throbbing wound that was her want for him.

'Yes,' he muttered deeply.

She felt the rasp of his jaw against her achingly tender breasts and then his mouth was opening over one darkly swollen nipple. Romney lifted herself, arching, her fingers tangling in his sweat-darkened hair, drawing his head closer to deepen the kiss he had been restraining. His hand stroked erotically along her silken inner thigh and soft little cries came unceasingly from her as his lips and tongue did incredibly voluptuous things to first one nipple and then the other, sensitising them beyond endurance, to the point of pain, but pain was pleasure and agony was ecstasy, and Romney only knew she wanted no end to this rapture, no end save the explosion she sensed was inevitable.

Justin lifted his head, moving to lie on his side, drawing her roughly against him, his hand gripping her hip, pulling the lower part of her body closer and closer, and excitement tore at her as she felt his swollen urgency, the hard demand of his body.

A strange violence had come upon them. They were locked together, straining to be closer, and convulsive shudders racked them both as their caresses grew almost hurtful. They were both panting, and sweating too, their skin glistening. Romney began to undulate against him in the eternal rhythm she hadn't realised she knew, almost grinding her hips against him in the violence of her need, and Justin groaned harshly.

He turned her on to her back, crushing her with his weight, and Romney writhed frenziedly beneath him, choked little sounds coming from deep in her throat, urging him to make her his.

His face was so close to hers. She could look
into the tempestuous depths of passion-darkened
eyes, and touch the stormy line of his mouth with
hers, and a powerful surge of love made her want
to weep.

If only he loved me!

It was the only thought she was capable of as
her hands strove to find a way between their
bodies and reach his belt, frantic to remove the
last remaining barrier between them.

Justin was moving to assist her when the
telephone beside the bed shrilled. He swore
violently.

'Leave it, Romney.'

'I can't!' Her voice was an appalled whisper as
she struggled to sit up, all the conditioning of a
year making her instantly obedient to the
clamorous sound. 'It will be Kit ... I must
answer!'

She saw the bitter anger in his eyes as she picked
up the receiver.

'Romney, I want you.' Kit's voice was faint and
agonised, but she knew Justin heard it as clearly as
she did.

'I'll come,' she promised unevenly.

'Hurry!'

'Yes.' She put down the receiver and looked in
anguish at Justin, lifting one shaking hand to push
her tangled hair back from her hot wet face. 'He
needs me.'

'And I don't, I suppose?' he challenged
caustically.

She winced, struck suddenly by the selfishness of
both brothers. It was always their own needs that
mattered, never hers.

'I'm sorry,' she said tiredly, hopelessly.

'Don't go to him, Romney.' Justin's tone was softer.

'I have to.'

She was wasting valuable moments, she realised, getting up off the bed and searching for her crimson robe. Later there would be time for remorse over her near-betrayal of Kit ... No, she couldn't exonerate herself with that qualification. She had already betrayed him even if the final act hadn't occurred. She had intended it to. If he hadn't rung through just then, Justin might even now be possessing her.

She had enough presence of mind to realise that she must wear a nightdress under her robe or arouse Kit's suspicions—and he must never know. Knowing would destroy him. She pulled the brief white garment over her head and Justin watched her bitterly, seated now on the edge of the bed.

'How can you do it?' he demanded violently. 'How can you go to him, let him touch you, after how ... after the way we've just ... been, together?'

'You don't understand.' Hurriedly she dragged on the beautiful robe, belting it tightly.

'I think I'm beginning to.' His mouth twisted as he stood up. 'When he made such an issue out of returning to his room alone, insisting you stayed for coffee, you thought it meant he wouldn't be wanting you tonight. And you can't bear to spend a night without a man, can you, you little bitch? That's why you made so few protests when you knew I intended making love to you ... Any man is better than none! But now Kit has changed his mind, and so you're going to him ... Because, let's give you some credit, you do love him and you didn't want to have to be unfaithful to him. He had forced it on you, but now he's rescued you from having to betray him ... You're just naturally promiscuous, I suppose. You must have a man. Damn you, Romney ... Tart is too good a word for you.'

'I can't—I have to go! Kit is waiting ...' White-faced, she found her room key and slipped it into the pocket of her robe. 'Make sure the door locks when you leave.'

It was a Yale-type lock, fortunately, so she could leave without waiting for him, running the few metres to Kit's door. His own lock was always kept clicked back if he was alone as his headaches were often so debilitating that he was unable to leave his bed.

She saw at once that he had no headache tonight. 'What kept you?' he enquired mildly, smiling calmly. 'Or who?'

'Kit ...?'

'Was I in time?' he asked gently.

'What are you talking about?'

Malicious amusement lurked in the blue eyes as he put out a hand to touch her inner arm. 'Your skin is damp and your mouth ... Romney, have you looked in a mirror?' His face hardened momentarily. 'Has he ... had you?'

'You ... knew!' Shamed colour flooded her face and she looked wildly at the wall, wondering if he could have heard somehow and knowing it was impossible. As Justin had mentioned earlier, these rooms were perfectly soundproof. The hotel would hardly have either its first-class reputation or its official rating if they weren't.

'I know my brother,' Kit said serenely, but his voice sharpened as he went on. 'I need to know, Romney. Was I too late?'

'No. You weren't too late,' she assured him dully, her colour still high. 'You set us up, didn't you?'

'Yes,' he confirmed very softly.

'Kit, if he had known the truth——'

'Ah, but that would give me an unfair advantage,' he reminded her. 'We have to ... contest on equal terms.'

'But to manipulate people like that!' she protested in a hushed voice. 'It's gross!'

'Think of the risk I was taking, Romney.' He laughed. 'I was terrified he might have taken you to his room.'

She had nothing to say. Humiliated, she walked round the room-divider into the little lounge and sank down on to the settee, burying her face in her hands.

After a minute, she was aware of Kit joining her, sitting down beside her and putting an arm about her shoulders, drawing her close.

'I'm sorry, Kit,' she said piteously, looking up at him. 'I did come when you called, though.'

'Yes, you came,' he agreed musingly. 'Poor Romney, it wasn't fair of me, was it?'

'I'm glad you called,' she told him fervently, clinging to him. 'I don't know how I ever ... He doesn't love me. He said I was promiscuous.'

'Then he's a fool. Joan of Arc herself would have swooned into his arms.' Kit sounded proud of his brother's attraction.

'Oh, Kit.' Sighing, she laid her head on his shoulder.

'Are you crying?' He sounded startled.

'Yes.'

'But you never cry! I'm the one who cries!'

'Ah, Kit!' Romney's voice was muffled. 'I'm sorry to disappoint you, but as a human being, I'm far weaker than you are. I would never have the strength to manipulate people as you have, or to take the risk that you have done. But I don't know why I——'

'Poor Rom. Do you——' Kit stopped.

The question wasn't important, but he thought he knew the answer. If Justin had never been wrong in his life, he was wrong about Romney now. Anyway, it was only a matter of time now. He felt curiously elated. Altogether, it had been a satisfactory night's experiment and now there was this unexpected bonus. It was a novel experience to be offering comfort instead of seeking it.

He kept his arms round her shaking form and massaged her back with one hand, just as if she were a baby he was trying to burp.

'Just tell me one thing, my angel-girl,' he murmured. 'Tell me you love me.'

'I do!' she exclaimed vehemently. 'Oh, Kit, I do, I do! And I'll miss——'

'That's enough,' he interrupted. 'That's all I wanted.'

Presently he raised her and led her back to his bed, drawing her down into his arms and continuing to hold her until she was still, his lips moving against her brow and temples, his hand stroking up and down her spine.

She slept with such a sad face, he thought, and turned out the light to protect himself from the implicit reproach.

But he laughed a little before he too slept, because the thought that had occurred to him was so very Freudian: it seemed to him that, for Justin and his father to have loved her to such an irrational extent, his mother must have been someone like Romney.

Only, Justin knew better now and had done for years, as he had admitted this afternoon. With a contented smile, Kit fell asleep, and neither he nor Romney could know that they looked like a pair of children who, in weariness and fear, had sought comfort in clinging to each other and found solace in the sweet oblivion of sleep.

When Romney woke up she was alone— surprisingly, because it was not late, and Kit needed to be really motivated to get up early.

She returned to her own suite and showered, washing her hair at the same time, her mind mercifully blank except that she knew she dreaded the day ahead. She dressed in white shorts and a sleeveless hyacinth-blue vest that flattered her tan.

She and Kit usually breakfasted in the coffee shop so she walked there, slowly, still nervous of the confrontations that lay ahead.

For once, the array of exotic fruits at the buffet failed to tempt her. She wanted the comfort of cornflakes; they reminded her of her mother and it was like going back to the womb, to sprinkle sugar on them and drown them in milk. She found an empty table and sat down, drinking her orange juice before she looked around.

Justin and Kit were sharing a window table. She felt herself grow hot with the memory of last night's events. As far as Kit was concerned, she felt shame for her betrayal of him, as well as anger at the way he had manipulated her and Justin.

As for Justin, her emotions were too complex to be analysed, apart from regret for their mutual frustration and a simultaneous conflicting relief over the way it had ended, because he would never have been able to forgive himself once he knew the truth about Kit, and neither would she ... Plus, there was pain, endless and unbearable, for the final opinion of her that he had expressed.

A waiter appeared, asking her if she required coffee, and when she looked again, Kit was coming towards her.

# CHAPTER SEVEN

'Hullo, Sleeping Beauty,' Kit greeted her cheerfully, lifting her out of her chair and kissing her on the mouth. 'You're lucky my libido is functioning in such a dilapidated way these days or you might have woken to find yourself being ravished. Join me on the beach when you've finished, all right?'

'Kit——' Romney wanted to question him but he was gone, and she sank back into her seat to finish her cornflakes with little real appetite.

She wanted to run away a few minutes later when she saw Justin steering a deliberate course towards her. Her cup clattered into the saucer and she swallowed convulsively, her pulses fluttering maniacally.

He was wearing jeans and a white shirt with a broad pale green stripe across it, and he looked coolly virile. Romney flushed and tensed, trying to withstand her body's memory of the way his hands and mouth had explored its most secretly intimate regions.

'Romney.' His features were taut, more austere than ever, and she thought he would have liked to strike her.

'Justin . . . I'm sorry!' she said swiftly. She didn't know what else to say. There was nothing else.

'No, my dear, I'm sorry,' he corrected her sardonically. 'Sorry I ever got involved with you . . . I gather you . . . confessed all to my brother last night.'

'Oh, Justin.' Her lashes dropped to screen the agony in her eyes.

'He has been telling me about you,' he went on silkily, pulling out the chair opposite her and sitting down. 'Would you like to know what he said?'

'Justin, please——' she began to entreat, desperation in her tone.

'He begged me not to impose on you a burden of guilt,' he went on inexorably. 'He told me that you do love him, which fact I had already observed for myself, and that you wanted to be faithful, but that you had difficulty ... because you're just a girl who can't say no, aren't you, sweetheart, although, admirably I suppose, you'd like to be able to say it ... Only he phrased it in terms somewhat cruder than that. Would you like to hear how he described your concupiscence? Normally I wouldn't repeat such words to a woman but I'm sure a girl like you already knows them——'

'Don't bother,' she interrupted bitterly. 'I can imagine.'

'I'm sure you can.' Justin viewed her with an identical bitterness. 'So relax, Romney. From now on, you're quite safe—from me. If I attempted to seduce you, I'd be putting myself in the same class as those fools who try to press drinks on former alcoholics. From now on I'll leave you alone.'

'Yes, I think that would be best,' she agreed tightly around the ache of unshed tears constricting her throat. She was white-faced and shaking. She had nothing left, not even pride.

He looked at her in silence for a few seconds and then he gave a cynical little laugh. 'I suppose it's quite funny. There I was, thinking Kit wasn't worthy of you, but it's the other way round, isn't it? My brother deserves someone better than you, Romney.'

'Justin . . .' There was an agony of appeal in her voice but his eyes stayed hard.

'In future, if there's a night when Kit doesn't feel up to satisfying your appetites, you can look elsewhere, sweetheart. Perhaps Otto Adelbert will oblige, although I suspect the poor fool is so honourable he'd first want to put a ring on your finger.'

He pushed back his chair and stood up.

Sadly, Romney watched him walk away, knowing the futility of protesting. In his own distorted way, Kit had dragged her back into the safety zone with his lies and there was no point in attempting to defend herself unless she could offer Justin the whole truth—and that she was unable to do.

She experienced an urge to giggle hysterically. She supposed it had its funny side. She was branded as a nymphomaniac, when she had only ever desired the possession of one man, and that because she loved him.

She spent the day with Kit and the Elstroms. Annabel Difford was working and Justin had gone windsurfing off one of the Gulf's islands.

But in the evening she sat alone under one of the little thatched cones dotted along the hotel's private beach. Kit and Torben had gone ten-pin bowling, or so they had claimed although she suspected the real attraction was the hotel's—respectable—massage parlour next door to the bowling alley, and Helle was at the hotel hairdressers.

There was no dilemma any more, because Justin

had promised to leave her alone, and she sat quietly, letting the sadness seep through her until Annabel appeared with a young Thai waiter behind her bearing a tray on which reposed two glasses and an ice bucket containing a bottle of Australian Chablis.

'What a hell of a day, what a pig of a photographer,' Annabel sighed comically and sank into a spare chair, nodding to the waiter to open the bottle. 'I don't know why I do it! No, I lie, it's the money and the prestige that attract me. Let's get . . . ah, château-ed together, Romney.'

Romney laughed helplessly, liking her even more than she had the previous day.

'Oh, bliss!' Annabel twirled her glass beneath her aristocratic nose and tasted the little bit of wine the waiter had poured. 'For wine and movies, among other things, you cannot beat the Australians. Justin prefers French, but I'm an Aussie fan, aren't you? Maybe it's because I once had an Australian lover, but never a French one. Whereas he had a French mistress.'

She smiled brilliantly at the waiter when he had filled both glasses and tipped him, neither too generously nor too meanly, and cynic though he was, he went away smiling.

'*The King and I!*' Annabel raised her glass dramatically. 'Since that's what people always connect with Thailand. And why, I want to know, haven't I seen a single Siamese cat since I've been here. My mother breeds sealpoints as a hobby. I've seen moggies in abundance, yes, but not a solitary Aristo-Cat!'

'I believe there's an orchid farm up near Chiengmai with a whole cageful of them,' Romney ventured shyly.

'Then I shall go there. I do love your bikini.' Annabel laughed mischievously. 'Forgive me, Romney, you must think I'm drunk already. I always talk like a voluble lunatic when I've been working. It's such a business . . . And I'm so scared, you see. I want to ask you something, but I don't know how. I was going to wait until you'd reached the in vino veritas stage, but that's hardly fair . . . You're in love with Justin Faulkner, aren't you?'

'Is it so obvious?' Romney asked bitterly.

'Only to me and perhaps to Helle Elstrom. Men tend not to notice these things,' Annabel replied gently, growing serious.

'It's totally one-sided,' Romney tried to reassure her.

Annabel gave her a long considering look. 'Yes, well, I think I'll stick around when my assignment is over,' she said thoughtfully. 'You see, I'm also in love with him, and all being fair, etcetera! Which is not to say I'm going to bitch you up to him or anything like that, but until we see which way the wind blows . . . Although if he isn't in love with me after all these years, I don't suppose he ever will be. But then, I don't think he knows how to love.'

'Kit said something similar,' Romney murmured.

'Kit. Yes.' Annabel gave her another long look. 'Romney, I'm not criticising, but considering how you feel about Justin, wouldn't it be more honest to give Kit the boot?'

'Yes. But there are . . . considerations I can't explain—without disloyalty to Kit,' Romney confessed painfully.

'I see.' Annabel looked up and laughed. 'Well, talk of two devils!'

Justin and Kit were walking along the sand towards them, and Romney grew still with the effort it took to conceal her inner agitation. She had not seen Justin since their encounter that morning. She had thought, during the course of the day, that she had come to accept the situation, but now she realised anguishedly that acceptance would always be a conscious act of will, and that even if she could earn his respect and liking, she would still not be happy. Only his love would do. It was that simple, and that complex.

Her smile was a mere convention, polite and wary, her eyes guarded, as she and Annabel were joined by the two brothers, so alike and yet so different.

'Boozing again, you two!' Kit teased, halting behind Romney's seat and laying an affectionate hand on her head. 'Funny thing, Justin and I met up in the massage parlour. We got to comparing notes on various Bangkok establishments . . . Oh, but Justin, I never told you about Romney's little adventure in a Bangkok massage parlour.'

'Spare me,' Justin drawled with an icy glance for Romney as he sat down.

'No, but it was really funny,' Kit insisted as he too took a seat. 'We'd been told it was a place suitable for the family, which sounded respectable, so off we went, Romney only expecting to benefit her health. Well, we arrived, and there behind this one-way mirror were dozens of delectable Thai maidens and one old crone, all with numbers to make selection easy. Romney promptly takes the manager by the arm, her mouth becoming a thin line, and says, 'I want to see where it all happens' and marches the little man off on a tour of inspection, discovering neatly turned down beds in addition to those massage table affairs in each, separate, room. Later she was shown the 'family' side of the business and persuaded to have a massage. She emerged with her handbag still on the same arm as when she went in, and apparently she'd had the treatment fully dressed. Can you believe it?'

'Only with difficulty if I'm to compare such behaviour with what you told me about Romney this morning,' Justin asserted glacially, cool grey eyes flicking over Romney who flushed with humiliation, and Kit gave her an apologetic glance.

It was one of the cruellest aspects of the entire unbearable situation, that someone she loved so very much should regard her with such contempt. She had begun to feel his scorn with physical pain; there was that permanent dull ache of unhappiness in her breast, and a constant constriction in her throat.

'Anyway, Rom,' Kit was saying. 'I was telling Justin that you and I were thinking of a couple of days in Bangkok soon, and he reckons he'd like to join us.'

'I've got a few business acquaintances there whom I'd like to see. What about you, Annabel?' Justin turned to the redhead with a truly beautiful smile that seared Romney because it would never be that way for her. 'If we wait until your work here is completed, could you stay on for a while and accompany us?'

'Two minds with butter!' Annabel laughed. 'Because, you know, I was saying to Romney that I thought I'd stay on for a while after this job is completed. And I'd adore to see something of Bangkok. We didn't stop there on arrival, we merely whizzed through it after leaving the airport and came straight on to Pattaya.'

'You'll love Bangkok, Annabel,' Kit assured her, somewhat maliciously. 'And perhaps Justin will buy you a ring ... You can get some fabulous rubies and sapphires there.'

'Emeralds, diamonds and pearls are my jewels, Kit,' Annabel retorted calmly, while Justin looked at his young brother with dislike.

'Perhaps pearls then, but it's the wrong place for diamonds,' Kit went on irrepressibly. 'The rubies, though ... Romney wouldn't let me get her a big one, but I bought her those little earrings she's wearing today.'

They were delicate silver filigree drop earrings in the form of butterflies, each adorned with a single, tiny, very deep pink-red ruby, rich and glowing.

'Butterflies. How appropriate,' Justin observed unkindly.

'But she does try, Justin, as I told you.' Kit was in high spirits, refusing to be squashed, and Romney could only cringe inwardly and strive to keep her face impassive. 'But there's another aspect to Bangkok, dear Annabel. Every known vice is on offer, plus a few that were unknown even to decadent characters like Romney and me!'

'I suppose you sampled them all, in the greedy manner of children at large in a sweet factory,' Justin commented, his disparaging gaze resting on Romney.

'Not quite all.' Kit's smile grew dreamy and Romney didn't trust the wicked speculation narrowing his eyes. 'I've got something special in mind for this trip, but ... Well, we'll see!'

'I can't wait,' Annabel said lightly. 'I thought when I arrived that you looked as if you'd done some desperate living lately, Kit. I'll find out about changing my return flight.'

'And I'll organise hotel rooms,' Justin supplied. 'The Narai, I think?'

They left for Bangkok the day after Annabel's assignment ended, when her fellow-models and the famous photographer had departed. The journey took little more than a couple of hours in a car supplied by the hotel. A driver had been offered as well, but Justin said he preferred to drive himself.

Kit was wan and subdued after a crucifying headache which had robbed him of sleep until dawn, and Romney sat silently beside him in the back seat while Justin and Annabel ignored them and talked about people and places they both knew.

Romney watched the brilliantly shining paddies flash past, the water-wheels churning slowly, and even now in the eighties, the occasional patient water-buffalo was still to be seen, standing chest-deep in water. It was a world far removed from the vast throbbing heart that was Bangkok or the sultry sophistication of Pattaya, and she felt as if they were the intruders, cruising through in their speeding twentieth-century machine while all about them the cycle of the paddies proceeded at the same unhurried pace it had known for generations.

Lulled, weakened, by the desultory pace outside their humming capsule, she let her thoughts drift to Justin. He had been so cold, and so cruel, in the last few days, rarely missing an opportunity to subtly deride her. She wondered which had been the last specific occasion on which she had felt happy, truly happy, but she couldn't remember. It had been before her commitment to Kit, she supposed.

There was nothing to be done, save endure, and even the final fulfilment of her promise which would free her would bring grief.

She looked at Kit and saw he had fallen asleep. She put out a hand to touch his thigh, as if even in sleep he might be requiring her comfort, and then she noticed that Justin was watching her cynically in the rearview-mirror. She could guess the interpretation occasioning his scathing smile. He would be thinking that even when Kit slept, her craving for a man wouldn't let her leave him alone.

Defiantly, she left her hand where it was, scanning Kit's haggard sleeping features with concerned eyes.

She was glad they were going to Bangkok now rather than later. The responsibility was becoming too much for her to bear, alone and blindly, without an update on what it entailed. She could take fresh counsel at their appointment tomorrow.

Additionally, she always took a certain pleasure in their visits to Bangkok. It had aspects, other than those Kit had mentioned, which appealed to her, the foremost being its beauty. It was true that there was appallingly squalid poverty in certain areas, notably among those who lived along the Chao Phraya river and its connecting *klongs*, and yet even there, there was not the gross misery to be found in some Eastern countries, and the way of life fascinated Romney although she wondered how they stayed reasonably healthy when they did everything in the same river water, cooking and washing not least.

Then too, there was the constant sight of young shaven-headed monks in their saffron robes, sometimes being offered a bowl of rice by one of the respectful populace, but for Romney, the greatest wonder lay in such things as the massive, solid five-ton Golden Buddha, the subtly magical beauty and lyrical grace of the porcelain-encrusted Temple of the Dawn, and the dazzling splendour of the royal palace, all outshining any of the descriptions in the epic fairytales she had loved as a young girl.

They checked into the Narai and, after signing in, Romney and Annabel took a quick trip up a broad flight of stairs for a reconnaisance of the shops on the mezzanine level while the other formalities were being concluded, returning to the vast and magnificent reception area to find the brothers apparently at the tail-end of an argument.

'I've told you I'm taking Annabel to the Baan Thai,' Justin was saying shortly. 'You and Romney are welcome to join us but if you want to do something else, it's up to you. Only, don't expect me to be interested in that sort of thing. At your age, I probably was, but I'm not exactly a curious adolescent, nor am I frustrated. I'm too old and too well satisfied with my own life to find such a prospect even remotely intriguing.'

Kit turned away from him with a sulky expression, his shoulders hunched, and Romney knew a quick leap of concern. He looked like indulging in one of his petulant moods and the accompanying tension was bad for him, especially in view of what he had to face tomorrow morning.

If only Justin had agreed to whatever it was Kit had wanted to do—but Justin wasn't to know the harm his refusal could cause, and it had probably been one of Kit's sillier ideas, coming from the side of Kit which had been dominant in their days at college, a Kit who had looked under stones, fascinated by the sordid and the macabre.

She found out what it was a short while later when Kit knocked on her door and found her in the middle of drying her hair after a shower.

'No, don't switch that damned thing on again,' he ordered imperiously when she had admitted him. 'I want to talk to you. Did you hear what Justin was saying to me?'

'Yes, but I'm not sure what it was about,' Romney responded cautiously, willing to overlook his rudeness because she knew he was nervous about tomorrow.

'You know those so-called . . . clubs?'

'Which ones?' she asked sardonically. 'The ones where you . . . When you take a taxi-taxi to a lookee-lookee show?'

'That's it. I'm curious to see what they're really like.'

'Yes, well, I'm sure Justin might have been too, years and years ago, men being what they are, but there'd be something wrong with him at his present age. Thirty-two, isn't it? If he passed up an evening with Annabel in favour of that sort of . . . ah, entertainment,' she defended Justin. 'But you go, Kit, if you're really set on it.'

'I want you to come with me.'

She had thought she was broad-minded, but that shocked her, and she stared at him.

'Me? But Kit, it's not the sort . . . Girls don't go to those places.'

'Want to bet? Lots of women go along and have a good old giggle, I've heard.'

'But not girls like me.' The idea made her blush after some of the stories she had heard about Bangkok's illicit clubs.

'Why not? You're not afraid of a little nudity, are you?' Kit taunted. 'You've seen naked bodies before.'

'Obviously! I was an art student, remember?' And would still have been, but for him, she thought with growing anger. 'No, it's not the nudity in itself that worries me. Oh, Kit, why can't you go on your own?'

'I want someone to share it with,' he said pathetically. 'And since my brother has rejected me . . .'

'Well, wait until you have the opportunity to go with some other man who's interested,' she suggested thoughtlessly.

'Wait!' Kit scorned brutally. 'Romney, darling, for how much longer do you suppose I'm going to be able to take up that sort of opportunity?'

She flinched.

'God, Kit,' she began contritely, putting out a hand, and he seized the opportunity presented by her softening to attempt to coax her into agreeing.

'Oh, Kit,' she sighed when they were still arguing ten minutes later. 'I appreciate your need to get out and do something, but why particularly that? Why not something else? I'd quite like to go to the Baan Thai, you know.'

'Why? So that you can sit and look at Justin all night?' he flared jealously.

'No!' For once, Romney too was showing signs of temper. 'Because, as you very well know, I love Thai dancing, and I enjoy the traditional Thai food and manner of eating.'

'Damn it, Romney, you've always been so understanding in the past. Why are you letting me down now?' Kit demanded querulously. 'Doesn't it mean anything to you that I've got this ordeal ahead of me tomorrow? I need something to take my mind off it, a diversion, and food and fascinating fingers just aren't sufficient. Anyway, we've done that before. I want something new, a different experience ... I want my life to contain as many different experiences as possible, as many as there's time for.'

Suddenly his mouth was shaking like a child's and, with a rush of remorse and compassion, Romney abandoned her defence of her personal interests, taking him in her arms, sinking back on to the edge of the bed while he knelt beside her.

It wasn't too much to do for him, she thought, rocking him back and forth in an automatically soothing rhythm, just as if he were a baby. He was a very frightened person these days and, considering all that he had to endure, surely no sacrifice was too great.

He got these silly little ideas sometimes with regard to what he felt he wanted or needed, and then reacted in a manner out of all proportion and harmful to himself if thwarted. It was safer to humour him, and kinder at the moment, given the circumstances, or so she had come to believe, having no-one wiser to advise her and always conscious of the responsibility she bore in the shape of what little influence she did have over him. He was so dependent on her, and anything she did or said could affect him ...

As for this show, or whatever it was, she wasn't such an invertebrate specimen that it was going to corrupt her, but that had never been her argument. Her sensitivity was involved and an instinctive desire to cherish her own innocence, being innocent being a somewhat different thing from being unaware, which Romney was not. She had never been naïve, and she could giggle over genuinely funny sexual jokes, but her parents had taught her a sort of purity that turned easily from the sordid and the degrading, as opposed to the humorous, and her instinct to protect herself was very strong.

Her parents . . . They believed she and Kit were lovers, and accepted it, but even so, Romney knew that if her father could know what Kit was urging her to witness now, he would black both his eyes at the very least.

But for Kit's sake, she would suffer the abrasion to her sensitivity. Only, she suspected that Justin would disapprove, but that was a purely selfish consideration. He need never know and, anyway, he disapproved of her already.

It was an altogether depressing outing. The 'club' was situated upstairs in a building in a busy part of Bangkok, there was the danger of a police-raid, only Coke, beer and rice-whisky were on offer, the air-conditioning kept breaking down and so, mercifully, did the movie preceding the live show.

The show itself was explicit and imaginative, but totally unerotic and very depressing. Equally depressing was the audience, mostly male, with Asians outnumbering Westerners in a ratio of about two to one. She kept her eyes shut most of the time, inadvertently opened them once during the mindless, automatic finale, and felt as if she had lost her last illusion.

Afterwards she walked down the narrow stairs with Kit's hand at her back, feeling as if she had undergone an unanaesthetised operation for the removal of some vital part of herself. With a curious feeling of detachment, she realised that she was mourning her loss of innocence. She felt defiled, and so very sorry for those poor, pretty girls and that starved-looking young man.

'I'm sorry I let you in for that, Rom,' Kit said regretfully as they stood on the pavement looking for their driver, a shy young university student who used the summer vacation to earn money to go on studying by introducing *farangs* to this dark secret side of the Bangkok scene. 'I thought, from what I'd heard, that it would be funnier. Not very edifying, was it? It made even plain old-fashioned lust seem to have a certain beauty of its own, because at least it's a warm, impulsive, human thing.'

'I wouldn't know,' Romney said quaintly. 'I had my eyes closed most of the time.'

'Oh, you darling girl!' Kit laughed gently and bent to kiss her cheek tenderly, like a brother. 'I'm afraid that's my sex drive finally done for, though ... Oh, my God! I could swear that was Justin and Annabel who just drove past!'

Romney didn't care. She just wanted to get back to the hotel, and have a bath and brush her teeth. Then, perhaps, she would feel cleaner, less—tainted.

Kit paused at the coffee shop door, just inside the hotel entrance. 'I could use a Coke. You?'

'I'm going to my room,' she said numbly.

'Rom?' He looked concerned.

'It's all right, Kit,' she reassured him with a little smile. 'I did—I do—understand.'

She retrieved her key from reception and took the lift up to the floor on which her room was situated. When she stepped out, Justin was waiting for her.

'Where's Kit?' His expression was grim. 'Never mind, I prefer to talk to you alone.'

Romney didn't know what to say. She only knew that he was coldly, implacably, furious, and that she couldn't take much more.

The thickly carpeted corridor deadened the sound of their footsteps. At her door, she turned helplessly.

'Justin——'

He took the key from her and she experienced a feeling of *déjà vu* as he unlocked the door and steered her inside. In the light of the room, so much brighter than that in the corridor, he turned to face her.

'Did you enjoy the show, Romney?' he taunted icily. 'I recognised the sort of establishment you'd emerged from when Annabel and I drove past you and Kit a little while ago.'

She had little hope of averting his anger; she had little hope of anything; but it seemed to her as if her safest refuge lay in flippancy. She gave him a tight, bright smile.

'Why, Justin, are you one of those men who believe that women should be kept ... innocent? However personally experienced they are?'

'Yes, apparently I am,' he conceded tautly. 'Although I never realised it until tonight. But it seems to me that the world would be a poorer place if women stopped dreaming and became as cynical as men. And I'm disturbed, I freely admit it, to discover that even an amoral bitch like you should choose to attend such a show.'

'I didn't choose——' Romney stopped, realising she was about to betray Kit. 'Well, relax, Justin, there are still thousands of women out there who dream.'

She had been one.

'But the agony of it is—' Grey eyes grew blank.

'You didn't answer my question, sweetheart. How did you enjoy the show?'

'I loved every moment of it ... Those gymnastics.' Sherry-coloured eyes grew bitter. 'If you really want to know what I thought, Justin ... I thought, that can't be healthy; and I thought, there must be an easier way of earning a living.'

'Yes, for instance, like making some rich young fool fall in love with you and letting him take you round the world. That way, you can do it all in privacy, in the comfort of a soft bed, instead of before the eyes of deprived or depraved strangers.'

She didn't know how it had happened, or why, because she had never hit anyone in her life before, but the imprint of her little hand lay on his lean hard cheek and his eyes glittered silver with rage as his fingers dug into her shoulders.

'You think you know a lot about me, Justin, and most of it is wrong,' she managed to gasp breathlessly, despite her fear. 'But I thought you also knew the one truth—that I do ... love ... Kit!'

'And he loves you, poor fool,' he conceded bleakly. 'And the sooner he realises what you are and stops doing so, the better—for him. But do you know what the real hell is, Romney?'

'Justin——'

'That I still want you! That I'm slowly being driven mad with wanting you.'

'Then go away,' she beseeched brokenly. 'Go back to England. Leave Thailand.'

'Ah, no! No woman has ever dictated my movements.' Searing contempt added itself to the desire tautening his features and his hands dropped to her hips, drawing her up close against his own. 'Can you feel how much I want you,

Romney? Would you like me to make love to you tonight? I will, if that's what you want, and I don't give a damn for any guilt you may feel.'

She had turned to liquid, molten with desire, in response to the hard thrust of his aroused masculinity, but looking up into his face, she saw the scorn and hatred that still silvered his hard eyes.

'No. No, I don't want you to make love to me, Justin,' she said stiltedly, deliberately, and felt as if she were killing herself and damning her soul for all eternity. 'I only want Kit. He's ... kind. He doesn't look at me with disgust.'

'Yes, you disgust me, and I disgust myself.'

His mouth took hers in a hard, violent kiss, ravaging her lips in hatred and desire, but seconds later he thrust her away from him, so brutally that she fell back on the bed.

'Justin?' she managed as he reached the door, because she loved him, and his brother. 'Justin, Kit didn't enjoy tonight's ... show, either.'

He stopped.

'No, I know,' he said softly. 'He's my brother, so I know.'

# CHAPTER EIGHT

THE appointment in the morning was the ordeal both Romney and Kit had anticipated, exacerbated by the fact that Kit hadn't slept. He had sat in the coffee shop for most of the night, except when he looked in on a cabaret in one of the hotel's more exclusive bars.

Somewhat stunned, although they had been told nothing new, they returned to the hotel. Kit's face was chalky, his eyes sunken and hazy, and he made little protest when she persuaded him to take two of his new tablets and sleep for the rest of the day.

'Only, don't forget, we're going to La Rotonde with Justin and Annabel tonight,' he reminded her, and saw her blank look. 'Did I forget to mention it? I saw Justin when I went to breakfast this morning, and he suggested it. So wake me if I'm still sleeping this evening.'

'If you think you'll feel fit for it?' she began uncertainly.

'Of course I will!' Kit insisted rather sharply and she knew better than to say anything further at such a time.

She returned to the huge reception area, intending to sit there with a drink and watch the people coming and going. A hotel bedroom could be too lonely a place, she had discovered, where homesickness was apt to descend. She knew she was fortunate to have had the opportunity to come to Asia, and certainly she had found it fascinating, but a year was a long time to be travelling, especially when there had never been a day, however much she enjoyed herself, when she was entirely free from worry and fear.

Annabel appeared as she was making for a free seat.

'Romney! I was just about to ring your room and see if you were there. Justin has gone to lunch with some business acquaintances at the Oriental and I was just off to the palace. Do you and Kit want to come?'

'Kit is sleeping but, thanks Annabel, I'd love to.' She looked at Annabel's pale green sheath held up by shoestring shoulder straps. 'I should warn you, you'll have to hire a shirt there if you don't want to change first, because they don't admit women with bare shoulders. Last time I went, a month or two ago, they hit me for thirty *Baht* and the price has probably gone up since then.'

She herself was wearing a slim emerald-and-sky-blue printed cream dress with a thin matching short-sleeved jacket that knotted at the waist.

Annabel went to change and they took a taxi to the palace, travelling through Bangkok's Chinatown *en route*.

'You're not looking very happy today, Romney,' Annabel ventured when they stood in one of the palace's courtyard areas some time later.

They had wandered all round, admiring the typical Thai architecture and exclaiming over the exquisite beauty of dazzling gold and blue and red, and had taken off their shoes to enter the temple, before walking all the way round the long mural relating its story from Thailand's history, but for Romney the most fascinating part always lay in seeing the ordinary Thai people making their offerings at the temple and sticking gold leaf on statues.

'Oh,' she began deprecatingly, with an unconscious little sigh. 'I'm fine really.'

Annabel smiled sympathetically. 'I suppose Justin gave you hell about accompanying Kit to that place last night?'

'Well ... yes.' Romney flushed, not knowing what else to say.

'Don't be embarrassed. If men only knew the way women talk among themselves sometimes, they'd abandon their funny notions about our being tender plants in need of sheltering. All the same ...' Annabel paused. 'I'm not being disapproving, Romney, and the fact of some girls attending such a show wouldn't shock me. But you? What made you go along with Kit? Or didn't you know what you were letting yourself in for?'

'I knew,' Romney confessed flatly. 'But Kit persuaded me. There are reasons why I give in to him with what probably looks to you like doormat submissiveness.'

Annabel looked at her tense strained face and nodded. 'I don't really understand, but I suppose the reasons seem good to you. Was Justin absolutely brutal?'

'I suppose ... Yes, a bit.'

'He was so angry, coldly, violently furious.' Annabel's voice had dropped. 'I had never seen him like that before. Usually he's fairly tolerant of other people's ... ah, vices. I found it disturbing and, let me admit it, discouraging. Because there was that element of possessiveness in his anger, as if he felt you had somehow betrayed him.'

'Oh, no, how could it be possessiveness?'

Romney protested faintly. 'He detests me, Annabel. He despises me.'

'Well, all I can say is, he definitely seemed disillusioned.' Annabel sounded wryly resigned. 'And I didn't like it. From my own point of view, I didn't like it one little bit.'

Romney was quiet after that, attempting to analyse certain things. She didn't think that even wanting her could instill in Justin a possessive attitude, so Annabel had probably misinterpreted that aspect. But he had definitely been angry and, now she thought about it, there seemed to be a contradiction in his anger, because he had already despised her before last night. What he had observed then had merely confirmed his low opinion of her and deepened his contempt.

So he shouldn't have been quite so angry, unless his fury had really been directed at himself for continuing to desire her. It was a trait she had observed in him before; he would always be much harder on himself than on others because he set a far higher standard for himself.

That had to be the answer, because there was no other, unless he was even more like Kit than she had realised. Kit wasn't always exactly rational in his reactions.

She and Annabel parted on leaving the palace, taking separate taxis, as Annabel was going shopping. She had invited Romney to accompany her, but she had declined, making Kit her excuse. She was beginning to feel uncomfortable in Annabel's presence. Perhaps because she was older or simply because she had lived longer without hope, Annabel seemed to find it easy to talk lightly, with almost academic interest, about Justin's reactions to both of them, as if they were competitors in a fair contest, with Justin as the prize neither of them was likely to win, but Romney couldn't share her ability. They were all still too new and painful to her, love and despair, anguish and desire, and it hurt even to say Justin's name.

Back at the hotel she had a quick snack at the coffee shop since she had gone without lunch, and then went to take the lift up to her room.

She turned with a polite smile as someone entered close behind her, but the smile died and her cheeks paled as she found herself looking up at Justin, cool and immaculate in a lightweight suit.

She was assailed by an absurd impulse to flee, before she was trapped with him in this confined space, trapped and overwhelmed, but it came too late, because he had pressed the button for the floor on which they all had their rooms and the door was sliding shut.

The lurch in her stomach had nothing to do with the beginning of their ascent. The grey eyes were hard and contemptuous as they appraised not only her tense face but the slender curves of her body beneath the bright clear green-and-blue outfit. It was such a slow, insolent scrutiny, almost as if he were inspecting a piece of merchandise of inferior quality, and Romney's pallor was replaced by a wash of shamed, painful colour.

'And which particular ... vice have you been exploring today?' he enquired smoothly.

Her eyes fell. She wondered if he knew how he managed to hurt her every time they met. Did he do it deliberately? She looked up again into the taut unforgiving face and knew an uncharacteristic urge to hit back, wounding him as he always did her, although she knew it was futile. He was impervious. She could never hurt him.

'Oh, nothing too off-beat,' she told him flippantly, her smile tight although her pulses were fluttering with unnerving rapidity. 'Just getting to grips with a Thai boxer. Steamy but not seamy.'

'Romney——'

She laughed, with genuine amusement, because he had looked so startled. 'No, I've just been to the royal palace with Annabel, nothing else.'

'And Kit?'

'Sleeping.' Her face closed.

'Ah!' His mouth curved without humour. 'Exhausted after trying to satisfy you last night? I thought he had a somewhat shattered look when I saw him this morning.'

'Justin——' she whispered anguishedly, but he didn't heed the appeal.

'You know, Romney,' he mused in a soft, silken voice that melted her bones and made her quiver. 'It seems to me that I'd be doing my brother a favour if I did take you away from him. He's not man enough for your appetites, obviously, judging by his permanently exhausted look. No wonder you have separate rooms. He must live for the peace of being alone.'

'How can you ... How can you say these terrible things? To me?'

Quaintly, she was indignant. Last night she had seen what was unfit for her eyes; now he was forcing her to hear what was unfit for her ears, and somehow that was worse because the insult was aimed at her personally.

He laughed abruptly. 'Now, if I were your lover, sweetheart, you'd be the one wearing that shattered look when morning came around, believe me.'

Humiliatingly, she knew a sharp stab of sexual

excitement. His words had conjured a sense of what it might be like to spend a whole night in his arms, held close to him until the sun came up, that lean hard body devoted to her pleasure and she to his.

'You wouldn't still look like an angel if Kit were satisfying you,' Justin continued, speaking softly again. 'You'll look like a woman when I've finished making love to you, Romney.'

To her relief, she saw from the lights that they had come to their floor, but then Justin touched a button on the panel and the doors remained firmly closed.

'Justin, let me out,' she breathed, trying to subdue her suddenly frantic fear.

'Come to my room with me and let me show you what I mean,' he requested huskily. 'There's still a lot of the afternoon left——'

'I can't!' she cut in desperately.

'Why not? You want me.'

He was pulling her against him, his hands going to the backs of her thighs, her buttocks and her hips. Romney was pierced by a shaft of pure desire, unmixed with anything else for the moment, and she yielded mindlessly, curving herself in to the hard pulsing warmth of his body, her arms twining about him.

Justin's lower lip nudged hers gently, then moved back and forth across it for a time before his tongue began an erotic stroking that made her moan softly.

'Let me, Romney!' His voice had thinned and dropped still lower, becoming a fine thread of sound, barely audible.

'I can't,' she tried again. 'You know——'

'Why not?'

'Kit——'

'Damn Kit! Leave him, Romney. A boy like that can't satisfy you!' With a convulsive shudder, he pulled her still closer, leaving her in no doubt as to the throbbing urgency of his need and, looking up into his eyes, she saw the same raw, leaping desire that ran so wildly in her veins. 'I want you!'

'Why, Justin?' she asked impulsively. 'Why do you want me?'

Because while she could no longer question the truth of it, it still seemed to her unutterably miraculous that he should do so—when he could have women like Annabel Difford. Surely to a man incapable of loving, as he was, beauty, intelligence and sex-appeal were everything. And she herself was so very ordinary.

She saw the bitter anger that transfigured his face and his mouth twisted as he turned her loose. He pushed a button and the lift door slid open.

'What the hell do you want?' he snapped as he pushed her out. 'For us to sit down and attempt to analyse the whys and wherefores of sexual attraction? For that matter, why do you want me? Yes!' he agreed cynically on hearing her bitter little laugh. 'Because I'm a man and capable of satisfying you. That's the way we are, that's the way most human beings are, and it's time you learnt to accept it. You're only subjecting yourself to unnecessary angst by feeling that you should only want Kit and no-one else because he's the one you love. Grow up, Romney!'

'Justin——' She stopped. She would shock him immeasurably if she told him that the only man she had ever wanted was one whom she loved and wanted to share all her life with. Only, unless she was more specific, he wouldn't believe her. He would think she was referring to Kit and attempting to deceive herself.

And there was still Kit to be considered. Nothing and no-one was more important just now. Anyway, Justin didn't love her and couldn't love her, so it was pointless trying. She didn't want his pity, if he could be made to believe her, which was doubtful. Like Kit, he could be quite wilfully blind.

'Well, go to him, Romney,' Justin mocked harshly. 'Go and wake him and see if he can satisfy you... And I'll bet my life that when I see you again, you'll still look like an innocent.'

Mercifully, they had to turn in separate directions to reach their rooms, and Romney hurried to hers, locking the door when she was inside and sinking into a chair, shaking and feverish.

Her love and desire for Justin had become a perpetual throbbing ache, and frustration had taken the sweetness from it and left only the heavy pain which existed not only in the deep untouched heart of her femininity where she wanted him, but now spread throughout all her being, to her arms and her legs and even her brain. She was weighed down with it, unsatisfied, almost handicapped, because there was never a moment when she was free to be herself, released from the distraction of wanting him.

Dear God, how much longer must she endure this? Then the additional weight of guilt dropped down on her because she knew almost exactly how much longer, and knew too that the ending of that time, when she would be free to go home, would bring only grief—and no end to her need for Justin Faulkner.

\*　　\*　　\*

La Rotonde, as the little boxes of matches supplied in the hotel rooms proclaimed, was Thailand's only revolving restaurant, situated on top of the hotel, on the fifteenth floor, and famed for its French cuisine. It was both elegant and luxurious, offering a breathtaking view over Bangkok.

Romney dressed with special care and considerable pleasure for the occasion. She had learnt how to wear a sari in India, and this one was her favourite, soft gauzy lilac shot through with a fine glimmering silver thread. She possessed a number of various traditional Eastern outfits which Kit had insisted on buying for her at ridiculously low prices during their travels, and she knew she must make the most of them while she was still in Asia because, at home, she suspected, she would feel as if she were wearing fancy-dress, while here, they belonged to the scene.

La Rotonde offered every courtesy. When Romney and Kit changed lifts for the last part of their ascent to the restaurant, a sweetly beautiful Thai girl was there to escort them and once there, they were shown to the table where Justin and Annabel awaited them with the gentle, almost loving solicitude in which the Thais never failed, from the smallest urchin tenderly trying to rip-off a *farang* right through all the social spectrum. There was a rose for Romney, and she saw that Annabel, in a sleek white gown and masses of jewellery, also had one.

Justin had stood up when they arrived, and he bent his head to Romney with a taunting smile.

'No joy?' he murmured so that Kit, exchanging jokes with the waiter, couldn't hear. 'Admittedly you don't look like a nun, but you do look as demure as if you'd just stepped out of Purdah, which is virtually the same thing. And it's deceptive, isn't it? You're nineteen and you know it all.'

'And you know nothing, Justin,' she murmured sedately and sat down.

Annabel smiled at her kindly. 'Oh, you're not carrying a bag. I was going to warn you. I put mine down on the window ledge when we sat down and when I looked after a while it was no longer there beside me. Justin had to go back and find our original starting point to retrieve it. It just hadn't occurred to me that the whole structure wasn't revolving, only the floor. Justin said some very uncomplimentary things about feminine logic!'

Everything was superb. They all chose lobster for their main course and the chef arrived to cook it at the tableside, and the wine they had with it was perfect; likewise the other courses. The table was beautifully set, the candlelight romantic, and music was supplied by the very gifted pianist on the low central platform.

But Romney was unable to relax. A double awareness of Justin kept her tense: she was acutely, achingly aware of him as a man, and she was also unceasingly aware of his contempt for her. He could lacerate her with a single glance from scorn-silvered eyes. Agony lay in watching his manner with Annabel, the gentle teasing and the tolerance, the smiles that made his mouth beautiful and lit his eyes, so that his face became much younger.

With Kit he was alternately indulgent or irritated, but for Romney he had only scorn—and desire.

Because in addition to showing her his

contempt, every glance from Justin reminded her of how much he wanted her and challenged her to deny her own endless need of him. It was there in the smoulder of his eyes and the bitter twist to his lips every time he looked at her, and there was nothing she could do, no amount of will she could exercise to still the responses of her body. Always there was that stirring, the quickening of honey-sweet desire in her loins, and the all-over pulsing ache for him was ceaseless.

She loved him, and all joy was seeping sadly away from her, because without him there could be no happiness; the pleasure she had once taken in other unrelated things was diminished, over-shadowed by the anguish of knowing herself unloved. All that had once seemed important to her now no longer mattered. Nothing mattered any more, there was nothing to distract her . . .

Except poor Kit. Romney looked at him concernedly. He was trying so hard, too hard, determined to be the life and soul of the party, forcing himself to bring out an endless series of witticisms, growing outrageous if Justin seemed unimpressed . . . Like a child trying to win the attention and interest of adults when he fears he lacks their affection, trespassing over the limits of acceptable behaviour when he seemed to be losing the limelight.

Poor Kit, she thought sadly again. He so desperately wanted to win some sort of affirmation of affection from his brother and, too proud to beg for it, he tried to goad Justin into reacting.

And Justin loved him. She knew that, but Kit couldn't and wouldn't see it. Oh, they were both blind, and storing up so much pain for themselves and each other. Sometimes she thought neither brother would be satisfied until he had seen the other crawl, which was a measure of how many and how deep were the wounds their hostile relationship had inflicted.

She looked at Justin. Couldn't he see the too-bright look in Kit's shadow-surrounded eyes, the febrile way he kept picking up things on the table and putting them down again? His mouth had a tendency to shake and then grow very hard, as if he were placing himself under a strict control that he lacked the application to sustain, and he was obviously forcing himself to eat, although he drank from his glass of iced water over and over again.

Yes, Justin could see, it appeared, but Romney felt her heart contract as he turned his head to look at her. He had been watching Kit grimly, his eyes and mouth hard and, somehow, agonised, she thought, but now as he looked at her, his expression turned to one of searing contempt and she realised helplessly that he thought she was responsible for the way Kit looked.

Dear God, she thought, newly appalled, he really did think her something akin to a vampire, or one of those revolting spiders which devoured their mates.

Stiff-faced, she turned to watch the pianist, as she had been doing throughout the evening whenever looking at Justin became too unbearable.

Annabel Difford's glance followed Romney's and, perhaps sensing something fraught in the other three, the barely contained violence of emotion, she attempted to introduce an innocuous topic.

'That pianist is good, isn't he? He reminds me of

Richard Clayderman ... Plays some of the same tunes too. He's not a Thai, though, is he?'

'Filipino,' Justin supplied and something occurred to him. He addressed Romney and Kit jointly: 'Tell me, you two, what made you start your travels in the Philippines? It's curiously out of sequence with the trail you've followed since. You had to make that long hop to Pakistan.'

The effect of his question was startling. Both Romney and Kit looked positively panic-stricken, gazing helplessly at each other as if seeking inspiration.

'I'm not sure now,' Romney ventured breathlessly, frantically searching for an answer. What else was Manila famous for? Easter Crucifixions and—'Was it ... Could it have been the Film Festival, Kit?'

'No, you fool!' Kit's voice was sharp, but it softened when he saw her frightened look. 'I don't think the Festival was on when we were there. It was ... I can't remember either,' he concluded lamely.

Justin's eyes narrowed suspiciously. 'Some special vice or aberration exclusive to Manila, perhaps?' he enquired softly.

Romney flushed, but Kit's smile grew broad.

'How well you know us, Justin. But don't probe any further, will you? There are some things of which even hardened cases like Romney and I are ashamed.'

'I don't know why,' Justin suggested with deceptive mildness. 'Hardened, you said, so you should be beyond shame. But as long as you weren't getting involved in the politics of the region. That's what worried the old man when he heard you'd gone there.'

Kit relaxed, laughing with genuine amusement. 'Do I look like a political animal? Speak to Rom. She's the one who can sit up all night dissecting presidents and prime ministers.'

'I'd have thought you had better things to do with your nights?' Justin's eyes glittered over Romney.

And, treacherously, Kit said, 'Sometimes I think it's frustration that leads to vice. But I must say, an interest in politics seems the kinkiest of them all.'

Romney had never felt so alone. Even Kit had deserted her, in the interests of the deadly game he and Justin were playing. And how could she blame him? The contest had become crucial, and time was leaking away.

They returned to Pattaya in the morning and, as the days passed, sun-drenched days succeeded by purple heat-saturated nights, Romney felt as if the situation grew steadily worse.

And yet there was no confrontation, no denouement; there was merely a subtle, insidious increase of tension. Kit watched Justin, Justin watched her, and she—she tried not to watch Justin because doing so only served to aggravate the aching frustration and unhappiness that never left her.

She was only surprised that Kit made no reference to it, because his bright, too knowing eyes must have observed her condition; but all his concentration lay upon his brother these days.

Somehow, somewhere, she had lost Kit, but Romney was unsurprised. Justin had always mattered more to him.

It was the cruellest of ironies that they should all be so desperate and driven, here in this sultry paradise where the days seemed made for pleasure and the nights for passion. Kit was morbid or frenetic in turn, and somehow isolated, turned in on himself, in the phrase Justin had once used, because he was passing through a crucible that none could share.

Romney herself was helpless, mutely suffering as she watched the inevitable approach of a disaster she could do nothing to avert. She could only pray that it would not be the total disaster Justin unwittingly sought to make it, because if it was, she would be implicated, and share in his guilt, the guilt he would find so hard to bear.

It was no compensation to know that Justin too, in his own way, suffered. Daily she looked at him and read the tormented desire, and the contempt and self-contempt, all written on his tortured face, and her only reaction was to wish that she could give him ease, even if he didn't love her. But she could no more do that than she could give his brother life. To do so would be to put them all in hell forever.

Even Annabel was unhappy, she thought pityingly, strolling solitary in the hotel gardens late one night; Annabel, who watched and waited, for the birth or death of hope, and tried to pretend that it was merely a matter of academic interest.

Romney and Kit had been into town that night at Kit's insistence, to dine at Nang Nual and then stroll through the streets, pausing to bargain for useless trifles, and loving him, mourning him, she had been only too willing to indulge his silliness.

Now Kit was oblivious in an artificially induced sleep, but with no aids to her own repose, Romney paced restlessly in the gardens, knowing several sleepless hours still lay ahead of her.

She was wearing one of her little Thai silk two-piece suits, cerise tonight, and in the moon- and starlight, it was somewhat brighter than the surrounding bougainvillaea bracts. She supposed she was foolish to be out here; there was always the danger of snakes, but somehow she didn't care tonight. Somewhere above her, someone stirred on a balcony and went inside, closing the glass door.

Romney wandered on, looking at strange stars and the solitary lights that came from the Gulf, from the nearby islands, she presumed.

She paused, sighing audibly. The inevitable was so difficult to accept. That was the hardest part of all, to accept, and learn to be philosophical.

'What is it, Romney? Were you wanting me?'

'Justin.' She had tried to avoid being alone with him, but now that he was here with her in the sultry night, she knew that it had been inevitable.

'And even dressed for me,' he mused softly, looking at her. 'Do you remember? I told you always to dress like that for me.'

'I . . . I dressed for Kit!' she insisted sharply.

'Kit!' Justin seemed to abandon control, his voice harsh and condemnatory. 'And he has disappointed you and retired alone, is that it? You're destroying him, Romney, can't you see that? What do you do, threaten to find someone else if he doesn't satisfy you? Every morning he looks worse than he did the day before... You know, I hate myself, I despise myself for feeling this way about you, but at least by yielding to it, I'll be freeing my brother. Because you won't go back to him after I've made love to you, sweetheart. You won't want to... You'll have no cause for complaint. I have somewhat more stamina than Kit.'

'Justin, don't do this, please!' Romney beseeched huskily, close to panic, because if he touched her . . .

'But I have to, Romney.' He was reaching for her. 'Don't you understand that? I must! I must make love to you tonight.'

# CHAPTER NINE

JUST for a moment, Romney had stiffened resistantly, but with the feel of Justin's arms about her, his body touching hers, she gave up the struggle. Strength beyond her capacity had been required of her all through the year that lay behind, and the bitter conflict that had arisen with the arrival of Justin had imposed unbearable strain. This was her personal breaking point. The limits of her ability to endure were reached, and she conceded the fight with almost a feeling of relief, which was swiftly lost in the other turbulent sensations that assailed her.

Justin was trembling slightly and she began to shake in wild response. Through the thin layers of their clothing, she could feel the feverish heat of his body, burning her, drawing an answering hotness that came from inside where desire had started its imperative pounding summons. Her legs felt weak, quivering with the need to yield to his hard strength, and her heart was racing so that her breath fluttered between her lips in uneven gasps.

'Oh, Romney!' Justin's groan was agonised as he drew her closer, burying his face in her sleek scented hair. 'I think I hate you for what you've done to me, making me feel like this ... For the first time in my life I've found myself unable to control my desire, and ... Why you, for pity's sake? What is it about you ... Kit's dark angel, and my daemon. You haven't given me a moment's respite—I don't know what peace is any more. And you've achieved that, you, a greedy little——'

'Don't hate me, Justin!'

His searing resentment had lacerated her, and yet she could make no move to leave his arms because her own love and need were too great to be denied now. In a way, too, she felt compassion for him because so much of his suffering was needless.

'But I do,' he reiterated savagely, his hands merciless in exploring the graceful curve of her back, from shoulders to thighs. 'And I loathe myself. Do you know, I can't stand the sight of myself in the mirror when I shave in the mornings ... I look at my reflection and I see a man who has just endured a sleepless night, a man being driven insane ... And all for a cheap little nymphomaniac who is destroying my brother's manhood and torturing mine ... But the cruellest thing of all is the fact that even while you've obviously been wanting me as I have you—a mutual thing, Romney—you've still forced me to crawl. I don't think I'll ever forgive you for that, or for what you've done to Kit.'

'I haven't done anything to him! Justin, you don't understand, about Kit——'

'Hell, I don't want to talk about my brother now,' he interrupted scathingly. 'I just want—you. My way, Romney. It's going to be my way, this first time. You've done enough damage to me, you've humiliated me, which is something no other woman has ever done ... And so I'm going to win back some of my self-respect tonight. I will decide, and you will accept.'

Romney made no protest. She was deliquescent with love and passion already, held so close to him, and there was no room for anything else. She loved him and she had it in her power to ease the driving, tortured frustration of his need for her. It was sad, her own personal tragedy, but it didn't really matter that he didn't love her. Nothing mattered save that she could give him peace, and if she could satisfy that other need of his, to reassert his masculinity by taking her as a conqueror rather than as a lover sharing and giving, then she would do it.

That didn't matter either. She wanted him, in whatever way he wanted her.

The purple night throbbed about them. Justin's mouth was on hers, ruthlessly insistent, demanding and getting a response. Romney felt herself slide down into hot darkness, yielding instantly and fully, and Kit's last frail claim on her lay shattered and forgotten beneath the intolerable weight of her desire for his brother. She didn't even think of him . . .

There was contempt as well as desire in Justin's kisses, deep penetrating kisses that meant to take all of her to himself, even her soul, but Romney was beyond heeding it, beyond feeling humiliation. She was helpless and frantic in a tumultuous vortex of passion, driven and buffeted.

'My suite this time, Romney.' Justin drew back again, his voice shaking with the violence of his hatred and resentment. 'And if Kit wakes and decides he wants you and somehow finds you, I'm not turning you loose. You'll still be with me when the dawn comes.'

She was hot, and yet shivering, half-crazed with a wild excitement and the need to give him her love, show him how much she loved him.

Their progress to Justin's suite was continually

interrupted as they stopped to kiss again and again, until Romney's lips felt bruised and swollen, and to caress, touching each other's faces and bodies with desperate, frantic fingers.

They were both convulsed with desire by the time they stood facing each other in the softly lit suite, both panting a little. Romney's face was hectically flushed, her eyes like dark flames, but Justin was pale, his features taut and perspiration-beaded as if in the grip of an intolerable agony, and a little thinking part of her was shocked by the bitter passion that blazed in his eyes, inexorable and intent, while his mouth twisted painfully.

There could be no going back now, even if she wanted to. She had driven him too far.

'Justin,' she said huskily and took a step towards him.

He caught her in a tight shuddering embrace, his kiss a devastation that left her reeling. There was a remorselessness, a blind intent, about the way he set about removing every article of her clothing and her little sandals; and Romney's frantic fingers scrabbled at his shirt buttons while she moaned his name over and over again, twisting and writhing against him.

When she was naked, he pushed her quite roughly on to the turned-down bed, almost flinging her down, and stood looking at her for a moment, breathing hard.

'You never did tell me how you like it, and this time I'm not bothering to ask,' he grated tensely. 'It will be my way, for tonight, until you've compensated me for the hell you've put me through . . . My beautiful Romney. So lovely . . . and so sick inside.'

Then he removed his shirt, dropping it on the floor, and threw himself upon her.

The disaster was happening now, Romney realised anguishedly. They were in the middle of it and there was no way the final holocaust could be averted now.

Kit, she thought desperately, once, and then surrendered herself to Justin's demands. He was touching her, seeking and stroking the secret places of her body with hard, relentless fingers, and her own urgency was mounting, to an intolerable pitch.

She clung to him with slender arms, her hands clutching at his firm muscled flesh, then sweeping over him, her fingers shaking violently, her lungs tight beyond bearing.

She was consumed in the white-heat of his cruel passion. Almost savage he seemed, his hands kneading at her swollen breasts, massaging them, before his fingers curved round the passion-congested mounds to expose the darkened tips to his questing mouth. His tongue was a sweet torture, at one taut nipple, and then the other, licking and stroking, circling and pressing, until Romney cried out, a hoarse throbbing sound.

'Justin—please!'

His hands swept down to her hips and thighs and the darkness between, and his caresses grew so very personal that she felt her colour deepening even while heat gathered like a growing flame in the centre of her being, and intensified, making her molten, and her trembling fingers drove into his ash fair hair, trying to keep his head at her breasts.

But Justin was bent on dictating the course of their lovemaking and his lips followed the journey of his hands. Romney's head twisted and turned against the white pillows and a shivering cry escaped her as, with eyes tight shut, she felt his warm breath fanning her smooth thighs, and then his kisses, feverishly moving along their silken inner length. He kissed every inch of her eventually, even her feet, and yet kiss was the wrong word because he was doing more than kissing her—he was claiming her, marking her as his, and punishing her. She felt as if he branded her, making her forbidden to any other man.

'You see what you've made of me, Romney,' he accused bitterly, his mouth at her breasts once more. 'I've never been this way with a woman before, never inflicted . . . punishment. But damn you, it's a fit revenge for what you've done to me . . . Can you feel how much I want you?'

He was concentrating on her distended nipples again, and the flush of passion lay all over her breasts as his lips tortured the exquisitely hard peaks until pleasure became pain and her desire made a great leap to heights she had never dreamed of, so that she thrashed against him, pierced with need and totally out of control.

Then, in a frenzy, Justin jerked away from her to discard the remainder of his clothing and for the first time Romney looked on his magnificent male beauty. A sharp shuddering little cry came from her because he was so truly, heart-stoppingly a man, taut and hard, his body glistening with perspiration. She held out her arms to him, whispering his name . . .

For a few seconds, though, he merely looked at her with a faint cynical smile, studying the arousal he had wrought.

'You really are quite, quite wanton, aren't you?' Then they fell on each other, their mouths meeting with eager passion, lips crushed, grinding together, drinking further fuel for their passion from each other, and their hands moved on each other's bodies, frantically searching, discovering, exploring.

Romney found she was able to touch him without shyness. Somehow it was the natural thing to do, when she loved him so very much, and her desire to please him was as great as her desire to be pleasured by him. She was beguiled, utterly seduced by the evidence of his hard arousal, the way he shuddered as her little fingers continued their voyage of discovery, delighting in his rigid maleness, until he stopped her with a harsh strangled groan and lifted himself over her.

Instinctively, she parted her thighs to accommodate him, flinching a little as she felt him there, for the first time, because it seemed almost shockingly intimate, but then she felt the roughness of his thighs between the softness of hers and somehow the perfect, complementary difference between them seemed the greatest miracle of all and she went mad in his arms, crazed with the pulsating hunger deep inside her.

Then she felt his hands grasping her hips, lifting her to him, and as she arched in compliance Justin lost all control, gathering himself tautly and driving into her with a low inarticulate cry.

Romney had not really expected pain and certainly not the rending agony that ripped through her lower body and made her cry out in shocked protest, feeling as if she were being torn apart by the ruthless invasion.

But even already it was fading to become mere pain and there was sweetness seeping through her again, saturating her. She clung to him, shifting to facilitate his fierce passage, and the drenching sweetness grew sharper, moving towards exquisite pleasure as she began to move in harmony with the deep penetrant thrusting that seemed to touch her soul. Little frenzied cries of rapture were wrung from her and she pulsed against the pressure, moulding him within her, easing his possession.

And then, when he had forced from her those involuntary sounds and the deep rhythmic contractions of true ecstasy had started within her, he spent his seed in her as they beat upwards together in rare, towering rapture to receive their brief celestial gift before falling shuddering back to earth once more, exhausted and sobbing for breath.

Romney felt peace stealing over her, but there was something wrong, making her feel—sad. At first it was like a small fissure in the shining happiness of her mind, but slowly it grew deeper and darker.

Kit, she thought finally, sorrowfully. She had betrayed him.

Beside her, Justin lay on his back, striving to steady his breathing and swallowing convulsively, an arm flung across his eyes.

Conscious of a great sadness filling the room which such a short while before had been filled with the sounds of their ecstasy, Romney lay very still, waiting.

After a time, Justin moved wearily to sit on the edge of the bed, his movements slow and automatic as he bent and reached for his clothes.

'Justin, what are you doing?' Romney sat up, moving towards him. 'Where are you going?'

'To kill Kit,' he answered in a flat, lifeless voice.

He turned blank, dead eyes on her, but then his gaze dropped to where the sheet was stained with her blood and he winced and came to life. 'My brother . . . He let me believe—— No, he told me quite explicitly and in some detail! He boasted about your long passionate nights together, and how you . . . My God, he's a bloody genius. If he'd sat down and thought for a million years, he couldn't have devised a more effective way of punishing me for the wrongs he thinks I've done him . . .'

'He wasn't punishing you! He was testing us both—and now we've failed him,' Romney concluded sadly.

'I'll kill him!' Justin repeated violently.

In that moment, her only thought was that he was going to tell Kit, and destroy him——

'Why bother? He'll be dead soon enough anyway,' she claimed wildly and put her hands to her face. 'Now I've betrayed him doubly. I promised—oh, I promised!'

'What . . . What are you talking about?' Justin demanded.

Romney looked up at him. 'He's dying.' Her voice was like a thin threnody, filled with pain and mourning.

'No!' Justin's face seemed to sag, becoming haggard. 'No, I don't believe you! Tell me it's not true, Romney . . . Tell me!'

She drew a shuddering breath. 'I can't. It's something in the brain . . . I can't explain it properly. His doctor in Bangkok has the original report from the man he saw in England. He'll probably be in a coma for a little while, and then he'll die. We . . . we've kept in touch through his doctors in the various countries, with the experts

at home and in America and Moscow ...
everywhere, but there have been no new dis-
coveries. There's no operation for it. He'll have to
go into hospital soon, and then ... I think he
should be there now already.'

'But ...' Justin's face was grey and she saw
from his eyes that he was beginning to believe.
'Why didn't I know? Why didn't he tell me?'

'He couldn't——'

'And you, Romney?' Anger flared in his eyes.

'I wanted to, I thought you should know, but
... Don't hate me for this as well, Justin,' she
pleaded piteously. 'I'd promised him, long before I
met you, never to divulge the truth to anyone ... I
did try to persuade him to tell you ... And now
I've broken my promise, I've broken all my
promises and he'll ...'

She was weeping and he looked at her shaking
form for a minute before picking up the shirt he
had worn earlier. 'Put this on.'

He went to the wardrobe and extracted a cream
robe, donning it and coming back to sit on the
edge of the bed. He touched her knee, almost
tentatively.

'I think you must tell me everything now,
Romney.'

'Yes.' She wanted the comfort of his arms about
her then, but she knew he was incapable of
offering solace at that moment, when he himself
was so much in need of it. 'You know, when I first
knew Kit at the art college, I didn't even like him
much, but then one day ... He'd just had the
verdict from his doctor, and I felt so sorry for him
... He loves life, and he was so frightened,
especially of being alone when it happened, so I
promised him he wouldn't be. I promised him lots

of things . . . For a while after that he would have nothing to do with proper doctors, and we went to Manila.'

'The healers in the Philippines,' Justin realised bleakly.

'The first one we went to . . . Well, he did the operations publicly and Kit wanted to know what he was in for so we attended one . . . The fraud squad, or whatever the equivalent there is, arrived while we were watching. Apparently it was all sleight of hand. He was using . . . Well anyway, the next man we went to was, I think, genuine. He said he wouldn't touch heads or hearts, only the sort of things that those famous tennis players had cured years ago. I think Kit lost all hope then. He refused to go back to England, so we went to Pakistan; gradually I persuaded him to keep in touch with proper doctors, in case of a new discovery, or a spontaneous remission . . . Justin, there's not much more I can tell you.'

'Except how you gave up college, and kept faith, and let him lean on you and draw on your strength.' Justin's eyes were dark as he understood the implications.

Romney lifted a shoulder. 'Somewhere along the way I learnt to love as well as pity him, so there was no real sacrifice involved.'

'Then why were you still . . .' Justin looked appalled. 'This . . . thing, Romney? Did it make him impotent? Have you been so frustrated that——'

'Oh, no,' she said quickly. 'If I'd wanted him that way, how could I have let you? I've loved him . . . Oh, God, you've said it yourself, Justin. Like a mother. Or a sister or a friend. It was a deal we made, that he wouldn't try. He did occasionally,

especially in the early days, but I think he accepted
... He appreciated, he was grateful ... He had
other girls along the way, kind Asian girls. They
were the only other people he told and they cried,
he said, and refused to accept payment. I loved
them for that and so did he, because even pity is
better than nothing. It means that life—and the
world ... are still good. But discovering the
goodness has made it even harder for him to die
and leave it behind.'

'And you, Romney? I hurt you.' He looked at
her broodingly. 'And, God help me, I couldn't
stop. And I've said things to you——'

Her pallor gave way to bright colour. 'You
couldn't know. And, Justin, you must know how
... how it was with me, before and after the pain.
Only, I ... I've betrayed Kit.'

'How, if you only love him in the way you've
said?'

'Because I promised him!' She was weeping
again, silently, her dark head bowed with guilt.
'He wanted, just once in his life, for you to envy
him ... Instead of the other way round. I think
that's why he told you those lies about me.
Making you jealous was a kind of revenge, or
punishment, for your not loving him—as he
thought, but you do, don't you?'

'Ah, God, surely he knew that?'

'Yes, deep down, perhaps, just as you must
know he loves you?'

'Yes.'

'But he wanted a ... an affirmation. I think
that's mostly why he didn't want you to know
about this ... this trouble of his. So that anything
he won from you would be won on equal terms
and not because you felt pity or ... or guilt.'

'So really it is I who have betrayed him. I've failed to live up to his hopes . . . his expectations.'

'Isn't my failure to keep faith so much worse?' she protested, wrung with compassion when she saw his bleak look. 'I knew the truth, remember, and still I failed him.'

She tried to reach for him, putting her arms about him in an attempt to offer comfort, but he pushed her away.

'No! Kit may have needed you to be a mother to him, but I don't, Romney.'

Abruptly he got up and went to the cupboard, selecting some fresh clothes before going into the bathroom.

Romney lay down and pulled up the deep red coverlet, a silk and cotton mixture with a fine light filling, like a very thin duvet, and listened to the sound of the shower.

When he emerged, his hair was damp and he was dressed in charcoal grey slacks and shirt. He stood beside the bed, looking down at her in brooding contemplation.

'Don't blame yourself too much, Romney,' he advised abruptly. 'I think perhaps that Kit asked too much of you. When all is said and done, you're neither angel nor daemon—just a very human girl . . . And I put a hell of a lot of pressure on you.'

'Where are you going?' she whispered.

'I don't know. Ultimately, to speak to Kit, I suppose.' His eyes were haunted.

'Don't tell him. Don't tell him what happened,' she entreated passionately. 'Let him believe . . . Oh, let him believe we stayed strong. He needs that belief, Justin.'

'Yes. But you know, I think I have to tell him

that I know ... the other thing.' He sank to the side of the bed. 'I'm a swine. I'm only thinking of Kit and myself ... What about you, Romney? I hurt you. You screamed and I couldn't stop. I'll never forgive myself for that.'

His fingers curved round the side of her neck, his thumb brushing back and forth over her bruised lips, and she tried to smile.

'I'm fine, Justin ... It's something most women experience, isn't it?'

To her surprise, he coloured. 'Well, not quite in that way, unless they're very unlucky,' he said drily, standing up again. 'Stay here and rest, Romney ... Have a bath or a shower if you like ... Or go back to your own room if you prefer.'

'Justin?' she ventured achingly as he turned away and he paused, looking back at her. 'What about you? Will you be able to follow the advice you've just given me? Kit also demanded too much of you. You're only human ... a mortal. Will you forgive yourself or will you go on hating yourself?'

'Oh, Romney, I don't know,' he replied hollowly. 'I just don't know... Romney, is it really true? About Kit?'

She was silent and he left her.

Romney would never know what passed between the brothers. She did not see them again until midmorning when she found them sitting together in the thatched shade at one of the tables scattered along the private beach.

'Rom!' Kit hailed her as she hesitated.

Slowly she went towards them, painfully unable to raise her eyes to their faces, realising she did not quite trust Justin not to have told Kit what had occurred the previous night.

'*Sawatdee!* It's all right.' Kit put out a hand, pulling her towards him as he observed her apprehension, and his voice was kind and calm. 'So you told him . . . So, I'm glad, strange as it will seem. Thank you, love.'

She stood beside him, laying an affectionate hand on his bare shoulder, and felt the cruel talons of guilt clawing at her. With an effort she looked over the golden head to Justin, knowing that he must be feeling the same, in even deeper measure. The grey eyes were shadowy, haunted, his features taut. He looked back at her, and her heart twisted with compassion as she read his suppressed desperation. His lips moved soundlessly, in reassurance, she thought, although she wasn't sure.

At least Kit was happy now. A new serenity glowed in his eyes and kept his mouth curved, and she knew that his acceptance was complete. He had been given what he had felt had eluded him all his life, and it had been the only thing he had ever really wanted. Now he was ready.

'I've been very hard on you, on you both, haven't I?' he mused later when he and Romney took one of their slow walks along the beath. 'But that's over now. Justin told me . . . Well, he told me many things.'

In the days that followed, Justin behaved like a man possessed, trying desperately to find the miracle Romney and Kit knew didn't exist. He accepted Kit's desire to stay in Thailand, but otherwise he acted as if driven by devils. He went to see the doctor in Bangkok, and after that, spent thousands and thousands of *baht* on telephone calls all over the world, first to Kit's doctor in England, and then to medical centres all around the globe, furiously determined to find some way of averting the inevitable.

But no-one could give him even a shred of hope to cling to. Helplessly, Romney watched his growing despair as Kit's headaches became more frequent and more distressing. There was no mistake, and no cure.

'I think I'm ready to go into that hospital in Bangkok now,' Kit whispered late one afternoon, preparing for sleep after hours of agony when the pain in his head had made him sob in Romney's arms. 'Rom, will you . . . prepare Justin to accept it?'

'I'll try, if that's what you want,' she whispered forlornly.

'I know it's placing another burden on you.' Kit was contrite. 'But I can't face it, myself . . . He's having such a difficult time. It's easier for us. We've had longer to think about it, for one thing . . . But all his life, if Justin hasn't liked something, he has gone right ahead and changed it. If something was wrong, he somehow found the means to remedy it. He had a sort of absolute authority over everything . . . And now he finds himself powerless. Not even by cheating can he beat this thing. He manipulates life, but he can't do the same with . . . with death, can he?'

'Poor Justin,' she said softly.

'Yes. I've always loved and admired him, Romney . . .' Kit was growing drowsy. 'I never meant to make him suffer . . . quite so much.'

When he fell asleep she left him and walked to Justin's suite, knocking reluctantly.

'One moment!' he called, but it was some time before he opened the door, his face tightening when he saw her. 'Sorry, I was on the 'phone.'

'Oh, Justin,' she said sadly.

'What is it?' he asked abruptly. 'Kit? Romney . . .'

'He's asleep at the moment,' she told him as he held back the door, allowing her to enter. 'But I have to talk to you about him.'

'Come in and sit down.'

Romney walked past the wide bed where just a few nights ago she had known ecstasy and agony in his possession, and she winced, her eyes falling and colour flooding her cheeks as she felt guilt oppressing her once more. Justin's mouth hardened.

Taking a seat on the couch in the lounge area, Romney looked up at him and found him regarding her grimly. She experienced a sudden wrenching in the region of her heart and her mouth grew tender. He was crucifying himself, and this time there was no ease she could give him. He looked so tired, his hard face marked with exhaustion.

'Drink?' he offered, indicating the mini-bar.

'No, thank you.'

'Well?' He took a single chair, at right angles to the couch.

Her eyes dropped again. She was prey to a peculiarly personal kind of shyness with him these days. In addition to her guilt over having betrayed Kit, there was a sense of acute, shamed embarrassment, remembering how wantonly she had responded to a man who didn't and couldn't love her. She couldn't look at Justin without recalling the intimacies that had arisen out of their fierce passion that night . . .

Inadvertently, her glance had fallen on his thighs, the tautness of his muscles straining against the denim material of his jeans, and she felt the treacherous, tingling weakness of desire shooting along her inner thighs as she recalled the sensation of his against them, and an aching sweetness stirred in her, there where he had been and no other, where he had moved so powerfully in his strong, forceful possession of her. Even now, she thought guiltily, she could still go on betraying Kit by aching for Justin like this. Her mouth felt dry, and she swallowed painfully.

'Kit asked me to tell you that he feels ready to enter the hospital in Bangkok now.' She raised her eyes to his face with an effort. 'I think this afternoon's headache decided him. He needs the care of professionals now. He should really have gone in long ago, but ... I was never able to persuade him.'

'It has been a hell of a responsibility for you to bear alone for so long,' Justin commented, his glance lingering on the bruises below her eyes.

'I probably made hundreds of mistakes.'

'Kit doesn't think so.' He paused and sighed. 'He has told me ... many things about you, Romney, and you have made him as happy as it was possible for him to be. He has told me of your strength, and your kindness ... And also, incidentally, how it came about that you accompanied him to that ... place, in Bangkok. I'm sorry I gave you such hell about it, especially when it was my refusal to accompany him that caused it.'

'It's all right.' She tried to smile.

'Oh, God, Romney, I can't believe it!' Justin exploded with sudden violence. 'I just can't believe that all that life is going to go out of Kit and he'll never smile that damned satyr's smile of his again.

I won't believe it. He was meant to live ... I feel so bloody helpless. There must be something, somewhere, that will stop it happening.'

He saw her sad face and looked stricken. Torn with compassion and sharing in his distress, Romney leaned forward, putting out a hand in love and sympathy, but he hit it away.

'Don't, damn you, I can't bear it! Don't get us mixed up. It's Kit who has needed you to be a bloody mother to him, not me!'

# CHAPTER TEN

SHATTERED, Romney stared at Justin's bitter face.

'I'm sorry,' she managed gently after a few moments. 'It was only ... sympathy, Justin, because you don't have to be alone in this. I know how you're feeling, to an extent. I love him too.'

The look he gave her was almost trapped.

'You can't know how your generosity stabs me!' The words seemed torn out of him. 'Your kindness ... I know, from all Kit has told me, just how unrepayably our family is in your debt. You've lent him your strength, let him lean on you, you've sustained him with your love and comfort. Oh, your service to him is incalculable, and we should only be grateful. Instead of which, you've suffered nothing but pain and the destruction of your innocence at our hands. God, I think that between us, Kit and I must have shattered every illusion you ever had.'

She couldn't bear the self-hatred blazing in his eyes. Shyness slipped away as she gave him a contained little smile. 'And in one case you've shown me a reality far, far more wonderful than the illusion I had ... I didn't know, Justin, I never guessed it would be like that—so intense and so ... Ah, God!'

'Stop being so damned kind. Why are you doing it anyway? For Kit's sake ... I know you must hate me, Romney.' Justin's mouth twisted: 'But not half as much as I hate myself, for that, and for the betrayal of Kit. But you know the worst of it? That even now, when I know my brother is dying and how much he depends on believing in us, I am still having the utmost difficulty keeping my hands off you. I am sitting here wanting you, aching to show you the way it can be, without the flaws of the other night ... What the hell sort of a man am I, Romney?'

'A human one, perhaps,' she suggested quietly.

'Yes!' He gave a mirthless laugh. 'I don't think that in my arrogance I've ever quite believed it until now ... Now, when I'm hurting with wanting you and tempted, almost beyond bearing, so very tempted to fail Kit a second time ... And knowing I must not, if I'm to live with myself; knowing I must never touch you again.'

Romney had turned pale. Now she understood why he hadn't wanted her to touch him—why she must not touch him.

But never? Would he always regard Kit as having a claim on her, even after Kit's death?

It didn't matter though, because Justin didn't love her; he wanted her. He was talking about desire. The only miraculous thing was that he could desire her to such an extent, driven by the intensity of his need.

She stood up. 'I think I should go.'

'Yes.' His face had a ravaged look. 'You used to avoid being alone with me, Romney ... In future, if you keep on doing so, you'll have my full co-operation.'

Numbly, she left the suite, returning to her own, to begin packing for the move to Bangkok. She thought they would go very soon, probably tomorrow.

She had clothes strewn everywhere when she answered a knock at the door and admitted Annabel Difford, looking serious.

'Isn't it bloody? About Kit. Justin told me. Kit had given him permission, I gather.' She looked at the evidence of Romney's packing. 'Preparing for Bangkok? I'm in the middle of packing too.'

'You're coming with us?'

'No.' Annabel's mouth turned down. 'I'm going home. I'd be in the way. And I've lost Justin anyway.'

'Annabel——'

Annabel tried to smile. 'And I don't know whether you've won or lost him, Romney, but ... Well, this thing is between the three of you, and there's no place for me. I know that now. Always in the past, even though I've never extracted a confession of love from Justin, we've ... Well, got together. Habit, I suppose, on his part, but it used to give me a measure of hope. But this trip, he hasn't laid a finger on me. So that's it.'

'I'm sorry.' Romney didn't know what else to say.

Annabel shrugged and folded her arms. 'Hell! If you weren't so obviously unhappy yourself, I'd probably scratch your eyes out. As it is, I can only say I hope you can both find something in this—thing—not quite unbearable; some promise that one day there'll be happiness again. I wish that for you and Justin, Romney.'

'Thank you.' She wished it too, but knew it was impossible. One day, she would forgive herself for the weakness that had made her betray Kit, because it hadn't really been weakness but strength, the strength of her love for Justin. But he would never forgive himself, because he hadn't had the justification of love.

'There's one last thing Justin has asked me to do for him,' Annabel sighed, preparing to leave. 'He has asked me to tell his father, but not until he calls me and tells me it's over. He doesn't want the old man trying to come out here. He doesn't think Kit could handle it.'

'He's probably right.' It wasn't that important. His father's rejection had never mattered as much to Kit as his brother's apparent lack of affection.

Kit was admitted to the Bangkok hospital the next day and became an instant favourite with the gentle Thai staff, because he himself was now both gentle and charming, and quiet now when he was in pain, partly out of some calmly accepting philosophy he had wrought for himself out of the year's anguish, and partly because he was being administered stronger drugs in increasing doses.

Only Romney was permitted to witness his recurring panic. With Justin, he seemed to feel a moral obligation to proffer comfort. With both of them, he was still frequently querulously demanding, as he never was with the staff, often in a spirit of mischief, occasionally in earnest, knowing that they would indulge him. Sometimes he demanded to see them separately, sometimes together, observing them with eyes that could still grow bright and knowing.

'Will you cry for me, Romney?' he asked lightly one day when they were alone together.

'Yes, Kit, I think I will.'

'Yes, you're so nice, you probably will. Justin won't.'

'He can't, Kit.'

'I know. Will you ... Can I give him into your keeping, Romney? No, you've had to be my strength for so long, you don't want to be his. But ...' His smile was cajoling. 'Will you help him, love? It will be harder for him and, as I've said before, I never wanted him to suffer this much. So will you, please?'

'If he'll let me.' Her face was averted.

'Darling?'

She looked up and saw from his face and his raised hand that he wanted her to bend close enough for him to embrace. She did so, and the arm he placed across her shoulders felt weightless, so frail.

'My dearest love,' he murmured against her cheek with a poignant touch of the old blarney. 'How can I leave the world with you in it? You make it . . . The only place to be.'

'Kit.' There were tears in her voice.

'There are a couple of questions I could ask you, but I've promised myself that I won't burden you with anything more, and with both of them you'd have to make a decision between a lie and the truth . . .' He paused, laughing a little. 'But, Rom, think of this sometime . . . You were never mine. I held you because of your compassion, and through emotional blackmail.'

'I've loved you, Kit,' she protested.

'Yes,' he sighed. 'Yes. Tell Justin to come and see me.'

She did so and returned to the Narai, waiting for Justin in the reception area. He was silent, introspective, when he returned, and they scarcely spoke while they ate a light meal in the coffee shop. Then they went up to their rooms, on different floors this time, with only conventional words at parting. It was always this way now. She couldn't reach him.

The next day, Kit wanted to see them together. He was talkative, lightly inconsequential, but then he said:

'You know, when I was a little boy, I always loved the phrase, "with a gay laugh", especially if someone was in adversity. It sounded so gallant, somehow. Then I grew older and realised that "gay" had another connotation. But I still think it sounds . . . the way to go.' He laughed, but then his mouth shook. 'Only, I won't be able to do it because I'll be in that damned coma.'

'Kit.' Romney took his hand, trying to control her tears, and Justin was at the other side of the bed.

'Promise me, both of you,' Kit demanded fiercely. 'Promise me that, one day, you'll do it for me—that you'll laugh for me. That's what it's all about, you know.'

'We promise,' Romney said and although Justin said nothing, she knew that Kit was satisfied with the look he and his brother exchanged.

Later, as they left the hospital together, Justin smiled for the first time in days as their eyes met, and Romney was able to laugh a little.

'He always has had funny ideas . . . Different,' she ventured. 'He's——' she stopped.

'He's Kit,' Justin supplied, and it seemed to Romney as the taxi carried them back to the Narai that there had been a lessening of tension.

Four days later, Kit clutched feebly at her hand. 'It's getting so dark, Romney,' he muttered, and then, frantically, 'Justin! I want Justin, I want my brother!'

Not daring to leave him, she rang for the nurse who rang for another, and finally Justin arrived, and Romney slipped away to await him in the special room set aside for relatives of patients.

An hour later, he came to her, touching her lightly on the shoulder.

'He's in a coma now, Romney,' he said. 'Come

back to the hotel. You can see him tomorrow.'

In the taxi, she said slowly, 'In the end, it was you he wanted.'

'Yes. But don't count it as a rejection, Romney,' he advised gently. 'It only means that, in the end, he was surer of you than of me. He didn't need to see you, to know . . .'

'Yes,' she said quietly. 'Was he . . .?'

'Yes.'

He would never tell her, she realised. It was between him and his brother.

They went to see Kit every day. They watched him and then they went away again. They seemed to inhabit a private little universe, with Kit at the centre, the sun, and themselves, the nurses and the two doctors in orbit about him.

Romney felt Justin had accepted now, at last, and yet still he seemed to exist in some sort of hell, his face drawn and haunted. It had to be guilt, she supposed. She had forgiven herself, because she knew now that Kit would have forgiven her, but Justin was unable to find the same freedom.

'Justin, what is it?' she burst out one night over dinner, unable to bear the sight of his anguish. 'What did Kit fail to say to you?'

'He said it all, Romney. It's you—the things I don't know about you!' He looked up at her. 'Let me come to your room and talk to you, please. You know I won't touch you now.'

'Of course.' She finished her crunchy Thai-style fried noodles and waited while he signed for the meal.

They were silent as the lift carried them upwards and she could feel the tension emanating from Justin, the same tension she was feeling.

In her room, she offered him a drink.

'Brandy,' he said.

'Is this brandy?' She held up a sealed bottle that said Grand Marnier and his lips quirked involuntarily as he inclined his head. She poured it to his instructions, and a gin-and-tonic for herself, and sat down in one of the chairs.

'Justin?'

'How do I start, Romney?' he asked flatly. 'By telling you how much I love you?'

'No!'

He looked up at her startled exclamation. 'You didn't know? No, how could you? I never gave much evidence of it. But why do you suppose I was so brutally critical of what, so wrongly, I believed you to be—of what Kit, all mixed up and frightened, encouraged me to believe you were? I didn't want the woman I loved to be that sort of person. I kept hoping I'd goad you into denial——'

'Justin!' Incredulous, Romney let her glass crash on to the table.

'And how do I go on?' He stared into the depths of his own glass. 'Kit knew. I told him when I knew he was dying. It seemed to please him then, but later he regretted it. One day, after he had gone into hospital, he asked me if I still loved you. I said yes, more than ever, and he said "She's yours!" Then he laughed in that way of his and said—I still remember it exactly—he said that you had never been his to keep or give away, and he said that he had only held you because of your compassion and through emotional blackmail——'

'Oh! He said that to me too,' she exclaimed involuntarily.

'And he said too that anyone who really mattered to you could have taken you from him,' Justin went on. He set down his glass and stood up, pacing to the heavily curtained window, then returning to stand in front of her, his expression tortured. 'So I have to know, Romney. How far did I fail him?'

'I think you know what he was trying to say, don't you? That whatever is done in love can be forgiven.' She looked up at him, with peace beginning to replace the pain in her dark eyes, but then her voice grew small. 'Justin, did he know? About us?'

'I don't know,' he said abruptly. 'Perhaps he might have guessed, or at least suspected, but I think that by the end he had learnt a special generosity—probably from you, Romney. He wouldn't distress us by referring to it.'

'Yes.' She fell silent, remembering what Kit had said about some questions he might have asked her. He had been merciful. He had also, she realised, wisely refrained from playing *deux ex machina* at the end, merely dropping a few hints to help them find their own way out of the darkness.

'Romney.' Justin crouched beside her so that his face was on a level with hers. 'I don't expect you to love me, especially after the appalling way I've treated you, but if there's anything I can do for you ... Be for you? If you'd marry me, Romney, I'd be whatever you asked, friend or lover ... I don't care, if only I can have a part in your life, if only I can share time with you and try to recompense you for ... for everything.'

'Justin.' She put out a hand, just the tips of her fingers touching his lean hard cheek. 'Don't you know how much I love you? I've known ... since the first time you touched me, I think. How could I respond to you as I did and not love you? How else could I have ... loved you, that night?'

Incredulity darkened Justin's eyes. Then,

suddenly, he bent, leaning in to her, his face against the curve of her neck. 'Ah, God! How have I merited so much mercy? Romney, I love you . . . I need you!' He felt her slight flinching and looked up ruefully. 'Yes, I know, you're tired of being needed, of having to supply strength, but I have to be honest. I do need you, my darling, but when you're the one in need, I'll be there, I promise you, for you to lean on.'

Then, satisfied, Romney put her arms round him at the same time as his came round her, and they clung together.

Nurses weren't supposed to cry, but a week later, the gentle Thai girl who had been specialling Kit stood up, unashamed of the slow tears rolling down her passive face.

Realising, Romney turned into Justin's arms, weeping for all the bright golden youth that was gone, and he held her silently, letting her lean on him. She felt the tension of his emotion, the grief he couldn't express, and she slid her arms about him until, gradually, he began to relax.

Then, finally, she understood the equality of their need and their strength.

Later, walking out into the hazy sunshine of a typically sultry Thai afternoon, Justin paused, looking down at her.

'One of these days, quite soon, we'll keep our promise to him,' he said quietly. 'We'll laugh for him.'

'Yes.' Romney reached up to kiss his cheek.

The only memorial Kit would have wanted was begun, because already they could feel the little bubbles of promise and hope that would eventually dissolve into an endless stream of love and laughter.

# Harlequin Presents

## Coming Next Month

Available in June wherever paperback books are sold, or through Harlequin Reader Service.

In the U.S.
901 Fuhrmann Blvd.
P.O. Box 1397
Buffalo, N.Y. 14240-1397

In Canada
P.O. Box 2800, Postal Station A
5170 Yonge Street
Willowdale, Ontario M2N 6J3

# HARLEQUIN BRINGS YOU

## Janet Dailey

### ★ ★ AMERICANA ★ ★

A romantic tour of America with Janet Dailey!

★

Beginning in June, enjoy this collection of your
favorite previously published Janet Dailey titles,
presented state by state.